THE BUCK STOPS HERE

Morven James

Matador
Troubador Publishing Ltd
9 Priory Business Park
Wistow Road
Kibworth Beauchamp
Leicester LE8 0RX, UK
Tel: 0116 279 2299
Email: books@troubador.co.uk
Web: www.troubador.co.uk/matador

ISBN 9781780880655

A CIP catalogue record for this book is available from the British Library

Typeset in Aldine by Troubador Publishing Ltd
Printed and bound in the UK by TJ International, Padstow, Cornwall

Matador is an imprint of Troubador Publishing Ltd

My thanks to those who have encouraged me to compile and publish this volume.
And to you, the reader, ... if you are entertained, the final link is forged, the chain complete.

CONTENTS

WORKS AND PERSONS

The brown envelope protruded through his letterbox. It wavered in mid-air. Fell with a threatening thud onto the mat. Brian cursed.

It was his day off. He'd made plans. Big plans. He intended to relieve the fridge of its load of lager and spend all day watching the footie. Later he would send out for a takeaway. He hadn't bothered with a shower, or footwear, but had pulled on an old pair of jeans that more or less covered his beer belly. This he topped with a stained t-shirt, printed with the "fcuk" label, which with the help of an acquaintance in IT he'd overprinted with the more traditional spelling. He undid the button on his jeans. A man needs space to breath, he thought, *and* extra space for the booze.

He picked up the envelope, turned it over. He sighed. No mistake. The address was correct and bore his name. He ripped it open. Just as he thought, brown envelopes always meant one of the bureaucratic bodies. This was from Works and Persons and was headed:

Please check that the information given below is correct. If there are any discrepancies, contact this department stating your full name, date and place of birth and your National Insurance

*Number ... the date and place of birth of both your parents ... the date and place of birth of **all** your grandparents.*

He scanned quickly. Looked for something relevant without having to read all four pages. Then a date caught his eye ... the 25th, today. A glance at the first page told him that this letter had taken eight days to reach him. Eight days! Of course they had only posted it second-class, but who knows how long it had taken the department to actually get it in the post. He had thought that nothing could spoil his day and now his worst fears were realised. An officer from the department would visit him regarding vital information. Today! Well, he thought, so much for an easy day. He sat down, read the letter, but by-passed the niceties. He pondered the fact that, according to their records, his maternal grandmother was Polish ... well I never, he thought, nobody ever mentioned that. But before he had chance to check out this unknown fact, the doorbell rang.

Grumbling to himself, he ambled towards the door.

'Good morning ... Mr Ellis ... Mr Brian Gordon Ellis?'

Brian looked at the suit that decorated his Welcome mat. It belonged to a balding skinny man with a sickly sallow complexion and a straggly ginger moustache. Expressionless blue eyes stared at him from behind rimless spectacles.

'That's me,' Brian said.

The man looked somewhat relieved and took out an

identification badge that bore his photograph. 'I am George C. Brailsford, representative from the European Union, Department of Works and Persons.'

Brian shrugged. There was no doubting that this geezer was who he said he was. He opened the door wider and, with a jerk of his head, invited the stranger into his flat.

George hesitated by the kitchen table. 'Well, Brian... You don't mind if I call you Brian, do you?'

'Suppose not ... *George*.'

'Ah, yes, well.' Clearly George hadn't expected retaliation. 'Here will do nicely.' He pulled out a chair. Sat down. Positioned his large briefcase, expanded to its limit, at his feet.

'This ain't going to take long is it? Only I've...'

'No time at all,' George said as he took out his laptop. 'But first, there are some preliminaries that we need to check over. Do you confirm that all the information we hold on record is correct?'

'I suppose.'

'Well, do you?'

Brian shrugged. 'Yep!' There's no point arguing, he thought, I'll just have it out with me mother later.

George sat back. Looked over the top of his specs. 'Do you wish this information gathering to be carried out in another language? Any language within the current European Union is acceptable.'

'What the hell do I want that for?'

'There are certain protocols to which I must adhere.

Ascertaining the client's preferred language is paramount.'

'Hey, hang on,' Brian said. 'Do you speak all them languages then?'

'Not exactly.'

'I thought not. So what if I wanted to speak...' he thought for a second. 'Polish?'

'Then I would have to complete the appropriate forms and refer your case to another officer who is fluent in your chosen language. We in Brussels...'

'Ah! Now I get it. You're one of them Froggies, ain't yer? I thought you talked a bit odd like.'

'Brussels is in Belgium.'

Brian shrugged. 'Whatever.'

'And no, I am not Belgian, I was referring to our illustrious European Government of which I am privileged to be a part.'

Brian tried not to laugh. 'Let's get on with it.'

'Certainly. The department is very pleased that its policy of creating work for the populace has succeeded. I can now report that everyone is in gainful employment. So, Brian, are you happy in your work?'

'You must be joking! I ain't happy shifting boxes all day.'

'Oh, dear! That will never do. Contented workers are hard workers. If you find the job unsuitable, you will need to fill in form XJKWFP 73196 to apply for a transfer to more conducive employment.'

'Yer don't get it, do you? I'm not after another job.

This one's okay, I'm just not delirious about it, that's all.'

'Ah! I see. So you do have job satisfaction?'

Brian nodded.

'Fine. Fine. On to the next section...'

'Hang on, how many sections are there, how many pages?'

'Two hundred and thirteen pages in all, but one or two may not apply to you. For example, I think it unlikely that you will be planning to become pregnant!'

Brian sighed. Then he had a brainwave. Couldn't see why he hadn't thought of it before. 'I'll be back in a tick.' He ambled into his lounge, switched on the TV, changed to the correct channel and set 'record'.

Once he was back in the kitchen, he looked at George who seemed totally engrossed and was playing with his controls. 'What we waiting for then?'

George pressed a key. 'This may seem unusual to you, but we will commence with retirement.'

'Have you read me details? I'm thirty!'

'Of course, I am fully aware of that, but by forward planning, the department is more able to meet the requirements of all clients, in all countries. It is key to economic security that will lead to a more stable situation for each and every one of our European citizens.'

'Rrr...ight.'

'At what age do you plan to retire?'

'When I'm 65. I'm not working a day more than I have to.'

George looked over his specs. 'So, you are a dissident?'

'You what?'

'You do not intend to conform with government policy,' George said with a sigh.

'Look, mate. Whatever they says retirement age is ... that's when I retire, right?'

'I see. You merely misunderstood the question. On retiring, will you be claiming an increase for a wife who is dependent upon you?'

'Eh! How do I know?'

'Well, surely you must have expectations. Do you plan to marry?'

'I suppose.'

'Do you expect that, on retirement, your wife will have paid sufficient contributions to qualify for a pension in her own right?'

'Gawd-help-us!'

George shook his head. 'That will not do at all. Do you expect your wife to work ... or not?'

Brian decided that this George was a total nut case, although he knew he had no option but to go along with him. 'Yep!'

'Yes ... what? Will she work?'

'She won't work until the kids are older, I suppose.'

'How many children do you expect?'

Brian shrugged. 'Two.'

'Fine. Fine. That's what we like to hear – clients who fit the pattern.'

I'd like to fit a pattern on you, mate, Brian thought.

'Do you expect that your wife will predecease ... er, die before you?'

'At this rate, I reckon I'll go first.'

George clicked away on his laptop. Then he looked up. 'Now there are a few more questions relating to your retirement activities...'

Brian was beginning to lose the will to live. He nodded every now and then to keep the geezer happy. But his mind wandered. Was this George a real person? Or was he one of those robots you hear about. Let's face it, he thought, you never know what the government's up to these days, they could send a bleedin' chimp in a man suit for all we'd know. If I jabbed him, would he say 'ouch!' or would he give a metallic clang and develop a mechanical twitch. Maybe he'd swing on the lampshade and shout, 'Ooh, ooh, ooh' while he thumped his chest.

'Well!' George was looking intent, expectant.

'Well, what?'

George tapped his pencil. 'I asked at what age you intend to die?'

'How the hell do *I* know?'

'Dear me, this will not do. It is a very straightforward question, Brian. Most people do not experience difficulty in giving a straight answer.'

Brian stared into space, unable to think what to say.

'For example,' George said, 'how old was your father when he died?'

'Last I heard he hadn't kicked the bucket and he's 58.'

'Your grandfather, then?'

'He's 84 and still going strong.'

'I see. So we could say that your life expectancy is probably in the region of 90 years?' George frowned, started mumbling to himself. 'Of course, I will have to check the records of his male antecedents to establish their life span and extrapolate the information exponentially...'

I'm sure he's not right in the head, Brian thought.

George finally returned his attention to his client. 'Now we come to the important issue of health. Do you plan to have any major operations?'

'Not if I can help it!'

'That reply is not helpful,' George said. 'Bearing in mind your current health, your working environment and your extra-curricular activities...'

'Hey, watch it! There's no need to get personal! I don't go in for any of that kinky stuff. Course I know all the big-wigs are at it, but me ... well I'm a normal red-blooded man.'

George sighed. 'Shall we say that you do not expect to need any serious operations?'

Brian nodded.

'What about illnesses?

'What about them?'

'Do you expect...'

'Yeah, yeah, I get it. Well, what's the average then?'

George's eyes widened, he lurched back in his chair, but quickly regained his composure. 'I am not at liberty to discuss government information!' He paused for a few moments. 'However, I am quite willing to state that you have an average expectancy of illness. My superiors will find that answer acceptable, I am sure.'

'Is that it then?'

Ignoring the question, George continued. 'Do you expect your wife, or children, to succumb to any illnesses, or to require any operations?'

'About average, mate,' Brian said. 'Are we done? Only I need...'

'Patience, Brian, we're almost finished. We now come to the questions relating to domestic pets. Do you have, or are you intending to purchase any kind of domestic creature? This may include: dogs, cats, horses, ponies, donkeys, budgerigars, canaries, or any avian creature, goldfish...'

'Well, it's like this, mate. I ain't got no pets. I never intend to have no pets. Not ever! But,' Brian glanced at his watch, 'me mate will be round any minute now and he's got a pair of the biggest Dobermann pinschers I've ever seen. The bitch is in pup, so the dog's more aggressive. Protective, like! What's more ... he particularly dislikes strangers.'

CARDSHARP

Barney crooked his finger at the sepia photograph.

'That's my grandpa. Up on the wall.' A grizzled version of the barkeep stared down defiantly. 'Shot, he was, right where you're standing. Shot, by a two-bit cardsharp. I keep a lookout for those dod-rotted critters. They ain't getting away with it in my saloon, no sirree. They don't come back here. Ever.'

The newcomer glanced round. Leaned heavily on his left elbow. Edged his face closer to the barkeep, a questioning look in his eyes. 'That's what I heard.'

Slowly, a smile curled round Barney's lips. 'That's why you came, ain't it? To ask how I do it? But you ain't from these parts.' His coarse fingers strayed to his head. He checked that the macassar oil still played its part, enabling the thin brown hairs to hold hands across his balding scalp. 'Knew my folks, did you?'

The customer nodded. 'I often drifted through, in my younger days. In '49, most folk were staking a claim in the goldfields. Your pa stayed put. I knew your folks real well.'

Barney was keeping a constant eye on him and noted that his eyes hadn't flinched. He decided the man was honest. 'Well, pardner, my friends have a mighty fine way of dealing with cardsharps.' He smiled, bent forward, whispered in the customer's ear.

The man laughed. Loudly.

'Now don't you be so ready with your hooting,' Barney said. 'Ain't nobody gonna tell the tale after my friends get through with them.'

'Where'd they come from?'

'I ain't sure,' Barney said. 'Pa never would say. He reckoned some things weren't for talking. Leastways, not out loud. Heard tell as how my pa got real friendly with some Injuns, reckon they could tell the tale. I don't give no never-mind. My friends ain't ever let me down.'

The man raised his eyebrows. His laughter lines deepened. 'Indians?'

'Okay! Have it your way, pardner, but I ain't lying,' Barney said.

The customer remained silent, put down his empty glass.

Barney reached for the bottle. 'This is mighty fine bourbon. Let me refill your glass.' He took the timepiece from his waistcoat pocket. Ten-thirty!

Already, the sun was sending men and critters scuttling into the shade to hide from its scorching fingers.

'It's going to get real hot,' he muttered, 'hot, and drier than a dead snake's rattle. When the stage gets in, there'll be some mighty thirsty folks. Before they arrive, there's time for me to tell you what happened to the last fella as thought he could cheat honest men.'

★ ★ ★

'Soon as I set eyes on the stranger, I smelt trouble. He was wearing blue eyeglasses. Sure we ain't as smart as them folk back east, but them eyeglasses mean trouble in any saloon. He was tall and thin, bony as a maverick in a drought. Wore work-clothes and dirt covered boots, but his hands weren't calloused and grimed like any ranch hand. I bided my time, to be sure.

"Got a room?" the stranger asked.

A scar jagged its way down the man's cheek. I wondered if the one as carved it was still living.

"How long you staying?"

"Just passing through," he said, "looking for work."

Old Dan, one of my regulars, shambled in, sat at his usual table. Took out his deck of cards.

I reached for a glass. "You not working, Dan?"

"Not no more. When the old man died, we knew there'd be changes. But not this. That no-good son of his reckons I'm past it. Me? Past it! Sure my joints ain't what they was, but that's no cause to put a man out of work. Paid me off this morning, he did."

"That's mighty bad luck, Dan."

Dan shrugged. He eyed up the stranger, shuffled the cards. "You looking for a game, fella?"

The stranger pushed his dark eyeglasses further up his hawked nose. "Sure am."

I shook my head ever so slightly, certain Dan would be the loser.

The stranger tossed a dollar on the bar. "Rye. Bring the bottle and two glasses." Dan pulled his chair closer. The stranger dropped his bag under the table, kept it touching his feet. He poured himself three fingers. Skidded the other glass across the table and bowled the bottle over to Dan.

"Help yourself."

Dan filled his glass, glad, I suppose, of a change from his usual red-eye.

"Thank ye kindly." He held out his gnarled hand. "Name's Dan."

The stranger ignored the hand, swallowed the rye and refilled his glass.

Big Butch, a sandy haired farmhand, rolled in. His red hands held a piece of twine, at the other end his mangy dog skulked. Thought the world of that old critter, he did. Close on his heels was Stan, owner of the local store, smelt like it too: paraffin, leather, glue and grain.

"Howdy lads." Dan nodded towards the stranger. "We got ourselves a fourth, my friend here, name of..."

"Two more glasses, barkeep," the stranger said. Soon all four were drinking.

Stan wasn't one to hide his curiosity. He stared hard at the stranger. "You got trouble with your eyes, mister?"

"Sure do," the stranger said. "My horse went lame in the dessert. It was two weeks afore I was rescued. 'Blue glass!' That's what they said. This pair of dark blue eyeglasses was the only thing to save my sight."

Quite a long speech for the stranger! Then he took

off them glasses. His eyes was all squinted up, made him look as blind as a donkey in a dust storm. It had the desired affect. The other three nodded and clucked like three broody hens, as though they understood his affliction.

Dan offered the well-fingered cards to the stranger. "You wanna deal?"

"I've a rule," the stranger said. "Always start the game with a new deck."

He took a pack from his pocket. Passed them to Dan, who broke the seal and shuffled the cards.

Stan won the first game. Dan took the second. I was busy, but kept glancing their way. I knew how the game would go. Sure enough, my regulars were winning. Even Butch won a few hands and that took some figuring, 'cause the big moose ain't got no more know-how than that old dog of his.

The stranger shuffled the cards. "Time we raised the stakes," he said. "If you're going to win, it wants to be worth the winning."

There was agreement all round. Usually it's cents and dimes with Dan and his sidekicks, but the smell of big money sets a man afire. I knew what they were thinking: if the stranger wanted to give away his greenbacks, they'd willingly take them. Sure, they believed their luck wouldn't change with higher stakes. But their luck did change. The stranger won one game. Then another. It wasn't long afore he took every game.

I started collecting the empty glasses. As I passed

their table, I saw through the corner of the stranger's eyeglasses. The marked cards were as clear as a new-painted barn door, but only through those dog-goned blue eyeglasses. Back behind my bar, I fingered the cold metal of my colt. I was a wanting to get the stranger out. But it was too risky. I let the colt be. I've never known one of them sly critters that weren't packing a derringer somewhere or other. As always, I'd deal with it later. In my own way.

Their money dwindled. His pile grew. He cleaned them out.

"I'll bid you goodnight," the stranger said. He stood. Scraped back his chair. "I've an early start tomorrow."

He picked up his deck. Toted his bag. Swaggered across to the bar.

I reached for a bottle, swallowed my gall, and said quietly, "You'll allow me to share a good bourbon with a mighty fine player?"

He shook his head, offered no thanks. "I'll take a bottle of rye with me."

I took down one of my special bottles. Handed it over. As soon as the stranger hit the stairs, I called my son to take over for a while. He knew the score.

I always put those side-winding critters in the same room. The adjoining room had a knothole in the locked separating door. I went in there to check how it was going. The stranger put a chair under the handle of the outer door. Slid the bolt on my door. He took out a fresh deck of cards. Removed the seal. Still wearing that pair of dark eyeglasses, he marked the cards. Stuck on a fresh seal. There, in his hand, was a new deck, with an unbroken seal. Job done, he flopped on the bed. Then he took off them glasses and turned. Stared, with wide blue eyes, straight at the light streaming through the window.

Back downstairs the room was thinning out. I collected glasses. Cleared up. Ten minutes, that's what I allowed, afore I gave my friends the okay.

When I was a youngster, I used to sneak up to that room. My eyeballs ached, they were pressed that tight to the peephole. It scared the bejesus out of me knowing what pa could do to anyone that crossed him. After that I sure growed up honest, there's no two ways about that.

I knew the stranger would soon be feeling mighty strange. He would be thinking the room was tilting. But this one was a real mean critter and I was a wanting to see him suffer. I went back to the knothole.

Those double-dealing hands clutched his neck. "My throat's burning," he rasped. He released one hand. Reached for the bottle. Took another swig.

His eyes darted round the room. Maybe he sensed some kind of danger. His mouth opened but no sound emerged. He tried again. Not even a pip-squeak. I watched his eyes. He couldn't know why he was getting a fright. Then he must have seen them! His jaw dropped open. The whites of his eyes showed top and bottom.

His nostrils flared. He was as scared as a roped mustang.

I knew what he was seeing.

Joker jumped out. Stretched to three feet six inches. Bulged his muscles to give himself more substance. The remainder of the deck didn't have Joker's know-how to increase in size, or width, but they had other qualities that their leader didn't possess. Joker cavorted and grinned. He nodded. Two of Spades began the onslaught. Sliced the stranger on his hand. Another nod from Joker and Three of Spades joined in.

The stranger looked at his bleeding hand. You could tell, by the look on his face, that he didn't believe what he saw attacking him.

Sure enough the lower spades were all slashing. The stranger flung his arms about. Tried to ward them off. Ten of Clubs bludgeoned his right knee. Still the stranger couldn't cry out. The lesser clubs played him like a war drum. Left red marks and bruises. He tried to protect himself. Nine of Diamonds flashed her smile. Dazzled him. The piercing light reached through his eyelids. The choice was plain. He jerked his hands upwards, to protect his eyes, his livelihood. The slicing and pummelling continued. Joker stood by. Laughed, as he conducted the whole shebang.

The heavyweights moved in. Royal cards carried a sharper edge, a heavier cudgel. The full suit of diamonds dazzled him from every angle. Joker was in full swing. He beamed and chortled as he directed the playing cards.

The stranger managed to stand. He made for the

door. Tried to escape. Hell and damnation! I thought he was going to make it. But no, his way was blocked. Thirteen each of clubs and spades danced in mid-air. They thrusted and threatened. The blinding brilliance of all thirteen diamonds made him turn away. He stumbled towards the window. They continued the attack on his back. The window opened easily. I keep it greased and real smooth running. He waved his arms about. A live puppet, his mouth open-shut, open-shut, but no accompanying voice to entertain any passer-by. My special rye had worked well. Choked off his voice.

Joker nodded. King led his troupe of hearts. They squeezed. The stranger's breathing was hard and fast. Still he managed to hang on. King looked at Joker. Sought permission to go for the kill. Joker grinned. Ran a finger horizontally across his throat.

King slid through the stranger's chest. Clasped his heart. Squeezed with all his might. With his heart no longer beating, the stranger was easily pushed out of the window by a willing army of fifty-two. I ran to my window. The stranger was sprawled in the street. Bloody. Bruised. Dead.

It was a good result.'

★ ★ ★

Barney straightened up, reached for the bottle. 'Ain't you got nothing to say? No? I reckon it do take some believing. But I'm giving it to you on the square.'

The customer stared. Mouth agape.

Barney heard a movement behind him. 'Well, I'll be dog-goned. Hi there, Joker! I'm mighty pleased you decided to come and meet my pardner here.'

The customer made a sudden movement. His glass skittered. The last finger of bourbon sloshed as he began a hasty retreat.

'You ain't finished your drink,' Barney called. 'I was gonna introduce you to my friend, Joker. It ain't po-lite leaving without saying, "Howdy".'

THE THIRD EYE

She cradled the smooth stone, felt its power. It was the most compelling thing she had ever seen. As she gazed at its iridescence beauty, the vibrant reds mesmerised her, swirled towards her, pulled her into their depths. She gasped as the sulphurous intensity of a seething volcano scorched her throat. It then plunged her, shivering, into an icy vermilion maelstrom. It breathed life into her. She knew they belonged together.

The silk scarf that had held the stone caught her eye. She caressed it. Its strength surprised her and, as though by instinct, she folded it diagonally, put it round her neck. Then she decided to ask a jeweller to make a brooch setting for her stone.

For most of the following week she felt on edge, desperate, almost bereft. At other times, she hugged her secret close. Saturday arrived. Unable to wait even a moment longer than necessary, she was standing at the door when the jeweller opened up his shop. She paid. Then pinned the brooch to her scarf and vowed to always wear them together.

That night, she prepared for the planned late-night party. The brooch and scarf waited on the bed while she showered. Even then, they remained within sight.

As she brushed her hair one final time, she smiled, and her reflection smiled back at her. She had never felt so happy as she danced along the pavement to the tube station at Kingsbury. Baker Street was her destination. However, she had no recollection of the journey; no memory of anything until, several hours later, she was at Maida Vale, but not at the party. Her head throbbed. Strong spices invaded her senses. A ghostly timpanist played a tattoo on her eardrums. She was confused. Her thoughts whirled and swirled, as though some unseen tornado had reached into her mind and scattered her feelings to the four corners of the universe. It took all her effort to phone a taxi for the journey home.

★ ★ ★

On Sunday morning DS Sanjay Patel and his murder squad colleagues studied the scene-of-crime photographs. They noted the livid mark around the girl's neck, and the state of her clothing, which suggested that there had been no rape. But the strange indentation on her forehead caused most concern.

DI Mullion related the details of the crime. 'This girl was found at 23.42 last night in the car park off Lexington Street. She was probably a prostitute. Apparently strangled. It would seem that the murderer was prepared. He brought the means of strangulation, *and* took it away with him. There is, however, one strange element. Her forehead bears an oval indentation, twenty-five millimetres long and an incredible *10 millimetres* deep.'

There was an undercurrent of mutterings.

'There appears to be no fracture to the underlying bone,' the DI continued. 'Forensics won't comment yet. We'll know more after the post-mortem.'

Sanjay's thoughts strayed to the safety of his cousin, Kalindra. After the recent death of her mother, she lived alone in the Kingsbury house, having declined his mother's invitation to join their family.

★ ★ ★

Kalindra rummaged through her pockets and handbag. There were no tube tickets, nothing to suggest her whereabouts of the previous night. Her face crumpled in dismay, tears fell, unchecked.

'What's happening? Where have I been?'

The doorbell rang. She hesitated. Didn't want to see anybody. It rang again. The letterbox rattled.

'Come on Kal! Open up! It's me, Julie.'

Kalindra ran to the door. Flung it open. Pulled her visitor in. Hugged her.

Julie broke free and stared at her friend. 'Hey, what's up?'

'I'm so glad you've come round,' Kalindra said, 'I...'

'What happened last night?' Julie laughed. 'Got a better offer, did you?'

Again Kalindra hesitated. It seemed so silly. How could she say that she didn't know what had happened?

'I ... I felt ill. *Really* bad. So I came back home.'

'You still look a bit pale.'

Kalindra smiled. 'I suppose I freaked out a bit. I'm still not used to being on my own, especially when things go wrong.'

Julie nodded. 'Shall I make us a cuppa?'

While the kettle was boiling, Kalindra thought about Julie. They had met at work, become good friends. It was the bubbly Julie whose curly red hair and freckles dominated the party scene. She smiled. Julie was forever trying to boost Kalindra's confidence, insisting on introducing her to everybody, and complimenting her on her dark eyes and hair. Kalindra smiled. They were opposites in many ways, but she always wondered what attracted Julie to her. She felt so unsophisticated, childish almost, alongside her gregarious friend.

'I've got something to show you,' Kalindra said when they finished their tea. Hesitantly, she placed the brooch in her friend's hand. 'Can you feel its power?'

'Not really,' Julie said. 'But it *is* beautiful. Where'd you get it?'

'Come on.' Kalindra led her friend upstairs, to the box room. Julie's reaction intensified Kalindra's feeling that the stone had claimed her for its own.

'After my mother died, I found a sort of puzzle box in here. This note was with it. I thought it would give instructions.'

Julie read: *'For my dearest granddaughter, when the time is right you will know how to open the chest'.*

Then she picked up the box. Even though it was now open, there was still no apparent clue as to how Kalindra had opened the smallish, intricately carved chest. There was no clasp or keyhole.

'I became obsessed,' Kalindra said. 'Devoted all my free time to solving the puzzle. For thirteen days! I even checked the box over with a magnifying glass.'

'But you didn't think to call me!'

'Sorry, but there was something ... well, something compelling. I had to be the one to solve its secret.'

'Go on then, how'd you do it?'

'I saw hieroglyphics along one edge. Recognised the Hindi script of my father's family. I wondered whether to ask Sanjay, but, like I said, some inner voice convinced me that the box was for me alone.'

'You could have called me *and* Sanjay ... you know I fancy that cousin of yours,' Julie said.

Kalindra remembered when she first held the box. As she had daydreamed, her fingers traced one of the carved figures. There was a movement. A small section protruded. Exhilarated, she inserted her fingernail into the gap. Nothing happened. The tactile box responded to her continued caresses, allowed her thumb to slide gently against one of the carved figures. She heard a click. A narrow drawer opened. Disappointment flooded its emptiness.

Undaunted, she twisted one finger into the drawer.

Her spirits leapt when she found a catch. The lid sprung open, released a musty smell from within. She took out seven bindings of hand written manuscripts but was frustrated, unable to read the Hindi script. She opened the yellowed newspaper cuttings, glanced at the photographs of a statuette. For no apparent reason a shudder snaked through her. One word leapt out: *Kāli* – the goddess whose name, unbeknown to Kalindra, had once struck fear into the hearts of travellers.

A click of fingers jolted her from her daydreams and she refocused on her friend.

'Hey!' Julie said. 'Remember me?'

Kalindra smiled absentmindedly. 'Sorry, I was miles away. What did you say?'

'How did you open it?'

'Just by chance,' Kalindra said. 'Then when I lifted a square of silk from the box, the stone rolled from its folds. There was a load of old manuscripts and some newspaper cuttings too, but they're all in Hindi.'

Again, she remembered thinking of contacting Sanjay who she knew could translate everything. Her cousin was now her only link with her past. The past, which she barely remembered, when her father's family traditions had dictated everything, even her naming. After her father's death, when she was four years old, her English mother no longer followed Hindu traditions. Now nineteen, and alone, Kalindra dressed and behaved in the manner of her many

English friends and colleagues. But the stone had recaptured her attention, its essence flooded through her.

'I got a jeweller to turn it into a brooch,' Kalindra said. 'I can't bear to be parted from the stone or scarf.'

Julie nodded. 'It looks great.'

They dismissed the writings. Cast aside the open chest, abandoned it in the box room.

Later that day, from the front window, Kalindra watched Sanjay walk towards her house. She knew that others thought of him as distant and standoffish. They didn't appreciate that his strict religious upbringing affected his communication with them. She admired his classic good looks. Revered his deep convictions and committed meticulousness. He was her dearest friend, almost an older brother or father substitute. He was someone for whom she felt deep respect and reverential love. She welcomed him into her home.

'Kalindra, you must not go out alone at night,' he said. 'It is not safe. A woman has been murdered.'

Confused, angry, she turned on him. 'I'm not a child! Don't order me about.'

The hurt showed in his face.

Immediately, she felt ashamed of her outburst. 'I'm sorry.'

He smiled. 'I am merely concerned for your safety.'

She knew he was genuine, knew also that unless she was careful there would be yet another plea for her to live under his widowed mother's roof, and therefore under his care.

'I'll take a cab,' she said, 'door-to-door. I promise.'

The next morning, at work, Kalindra's head started to pound. It soon worsened and felt as if a jackhammer was drilling into her skull. The undercurrent of noise from the large accounts office added to her misery. She constantly rubbed her temples and the nape of her neck.

Jules put a hand on her shoulder. 'You look dreadful. I'll get you a couple of paracetamol.'

When she returned with the tablets and a glass of water, Jules laughed. 'Got to get you fit for the party on Friday. If you cry off, it will fall flat ... that is if anyone comes at all. Who would the lads have to lust over? You're the tall, slender beauty they all want.'

Kalindra blushed. 'Thanks,' she said with a smile, grateful for her friend's kindness and thoughtfulness.

The tablets eased the pain sufficiently for her to continue working. In the afternoon, she took two more tablets, but they had hardly any effect. By the time she arrived home, she was feeling tense and angry, almost vengeful. She went to the bathroom cabinet. Searched. Cursed. In her haste, and anger, she smashed a glass eyebath and a magnifying mirror onto the floor. The packet was hiding at the back ... not surprising as she rarely took analgesics. She gulped down the tablets and went to bed. When she woke two hours later, her head still throbbed. For the remainder of the night, she tossed and turned.

'I won't let it spoil Friday's party,' she muttered the next morning. Then she saw the shattered mess. In tears, she slid to the floor. Never before had she lost her temper, or broken anything deliberately. She sobbed, wondered why she had acted so out of character. In her anxiety, she held both ends of the silk scarf firmly. Pulled downwards. The pain eased. Feeling a little more light-hearted, she cleared away the mess. Then smiled.

Fingering her brooch, she whispered. 'I knew we were meant for each other.'

Over the next few days, a pattern developed. During the day, throbbing pains gripped her temples and it became her habit to hold both ends of the scarf and pull downwards. Then, miraculously, by early evening they disappeared, only to return later. She became distracted, unable to concentrate. These phases increased in intensity. Developed into absences of awareness; short blanks when her consciousness had taken a temporary vacation.

'I can't understand it, Jules,' she said, as she held back her tears. 'I've never had headaches before.'

Jules handed her a tissue. 'Forget about it. It's probably just strain. We're all kept on our toes here and ... well, I suppose we do party quite a bit.'

'But I keep forgetting things,' Kalindra sobbed. 'It's as though something's eating at my mind. Eating it away. I'm going mad!'

'Don't be daft,' Jules said. 'Like I said, it's overwork and too many late nights.'

Kalindra managed half a smile.

On Friday, she remembered her promise to Sanjay and booked a taxi. She dressed, applied her makeup and then glanced in the mirror. The brooch sparkled its approval.

As she sat in the taxi her thoughts turned in anticipation to the coming party. Startled her out of her reverie, she looked up. Neon blades of colour flashed. Buildings crowded in, shimmied into unrecognisable shapes. A clock chimed – twice. Her brow furrowed when she looked at the driver. Before he had dark long hair and now ... this man was older, with little hair. But it wasn't just the driver. She remembered thinking how the red upholstery of the previous taxi matched her stone. This one was dark green. Her stomach clenched before it turned a somersault. Her hands shook. Fear grasped her heart.

'Where are you taking me?'

The cabbie laughed. 'Had a few too many darlin'?'

She stared at him.

'You asked me to take you to Kingsbury.'

Kalindra was relieved. She was on her way home, but fear stalked her thoughts. Shadows haunted her. How did she get there? What had happened?

On Monday, at work, Jules looked put out. 'What happened to you? It's the second time you haven't turned up at a party.'

She blushed, lowered her head.

'I see,' Jules said with a knowing smile, 'new boyfriend is it?'

'No. I... I couldn't make it, that's all. I'm sorry.' She was embarrassed. How could she explain those lost hours? Even telling Jules was too difficult. How could she expect her friend to understand?

★ ★ ★

Sanjay continued to be concerned about his cousin. Three weeks had passed. Five more murders. Word had spread to the tabloids. *Serial killer stalks London's streets*. Children were chaperoned. Women refused to walk alone. Horror haunted every corner. Terror trod the pavements. The strangulations were brutal, the oval indentations precisely in the centre of each forehead. Post-mortems showed no other damage to the skull of the victim. The media dubbed it *The Third Eye Murders*. There was no known connection between the victims, who included a teenage officer worker, an elderly cleaner, a known prostitute, a German tourist and a French au pair. Each lived in, or was staying in, different areas of London.

DI Mullion cowered in the lab doorway. Waved the report sheet. 'I need more than this!'

The pathologist beckoned. 'Come on. Closer ... she can't bite!'

Readily Sanjay obeyed. Mullion hesitated. Placed a handkerchief over his mouth before joining them.

'Look at her forehead. See the indentation in the bone?' His gloved hand pointed to where he had removed the flesh, left the bone totally exposed. 'It hasn't been done by force or the bone would have shattered. There are no traces of burning by heat or chemical.'

The DI moved away, his face already pallid. 'So? What caused it?'

'With a single occurrence, it could be a malformation. But you have five unrelated women with an identical mark. It's impossible,' the pathologist said. 'Oh, by the way, a slight trace of silk was found deep in the neck, so the ligature was made of silk ... a scarf, or rope maybe.'

As they walked out, the DI shook his head. 'What do you make of that?'

'It is rather strange, sir,' Sanjay said.

'Strange! Doesn't anything rattle you? How can I present this to the men? None of it makes sense,' the DI said as he handed the file over. 'You pass it on.'

That evening, at his cousin's home, Sanjay noticed Kalindra seemed preoccupied. He made polite conversation, gathered his courage for the important issue.

'Your grandfather told the family that you were blessed, a chosen one. He said he would speak again when you were older. Unfortunately, he died four years later. Your father met with a tragic accident later the same year. If either of them had lived, they would have ensured our betrothal. My feelings for you are constant, therefore ours will be a union of love, sanctioned by our forefathers.'

He hesitated. Hoped for some encouragement, but Kalindra remained silent, motionless. He bent over her. Saw the glazed lack of expression in her eyes.

'Kalindra?'

A hint of jasmine wafted up. He stepped aside.

She stirred, turned her head. 'Hello, Sanjay! I didn't hear you come in.'

'I have been here for some time,' he said.

He wanted to take care of her, to hold her close, but his moral etiquette would not permit such actions until they announced their betrothal. 'What is wrong?'

Her body shook. 'I ... I don't know.'

Try as she might, she could no longer fight her fears. Slumped in her chair, she started muttering. 'Has it happened again? Have I missed more time? Or was I asleep?'

In floods of tears, she told him about the headaches, the "absences", and the night of the party several weeks ago. The evening concerning the taxi, all the other occasions when she couldn't remember how she had arrived at a particular place.

'I'm frightened,' she said. 'It feels as if someone's manipulating me, changing my personality. What's happening to me?'

'You must see the doctor, tomorrow,' he said. 'Promise that you will do as I ask.'

★ ★ ★

The next day, even though an inner force seemed to urge against it, she took her cousin's advice. After careful examination and much questioning, the doctor wrote a prescription for painkillers.

'I have ruled out migraine. It could possibly be a mild form of epilepsy. I'm sending you for a scan,' he said. 'In the meantime, try not to worry.'

Two weeks later she returned to his surgery. He smiled in that quasi-reassuring way that doctors have.

'The results are negative.'

'What's wrong with me then?'

'I'd like you to see a psychiatrist.'

Her bottom lip quivered, her fears realised. 'You think I'm crazy?'

'Of course not,' he said. 'A deep-seated anxiety can affect behavioural patterns. It is essential to discover the cause. Hypnotherapy may help. For your own safety, we cannot allow this short-term memory loss to continue. Shall I make the appointment?'

'You don't think it will just go away?'

He shook his head.

Kalindra bit her bottom lip. She had an inexplicable feeling of dread and it was with great effort that she nodded her agreement. The doctor arranged an appointment for a week on the following Monday.

As she left, the inner warning grew stronger. It demanded that she stay away from this probing. Yet, she knew the doctor was right. She *must* find the cause.

The next day, during their lunch break, she sat in a

corner with Jules and blurted out her problem. 'I'm sorry, I didn't tell you before. I ... I just couldn't talk about it. I really did think I was going mad.'

'You poor thing,' Jules said, 'I suppose it didn't help, me getting on to you.'

'It made no difference,' Kalindra said. 'Nothing made a difference. I've seen the doctor. He has given me strong painkillers and he's investigating the cause.'

Even now, she couldn't bring herself to mention that her GP referred her to a psychiatrist.

Jules smiled. 'So, with you away, I reckon we'll have a girls' night on Friday then.'

'Of course not! I'll be there.'

She was determined to go. Even though something had contrived to keep her from attending the parties for these last few weeks. Something, or somebody!

'I already feel better. These pills are quite good.'

By Friday, she felt better than she had since the headaches began and was looking forward to her friend's party. She selected her favourite dress. Loosely tied the silk scarf, pinned on her brooch, and then brushed her dark hair until it gleamed. The red stone glinted its approval as it always did when she was preparing to go out. She felt happy. Excited.

'Even though I feel much better, I *will* keep that appointment,' she vowed. 'I must find out what is causing all this. Anyway, hypnotherapy sounds as if it could be quite fun.'

She checked her reflection. Twirled. Then clasped

her brooch. She felt its power. But the brooch seemed to warn her against seeing the psychiatrist. Her stomach kept pinching, niggling. It was as though the stone didn't want anything to intrude upon their intimacy. She couldn't understand why it was trying to influence her, why it was so against the hypnotherapy. It didn't seem to make any sense. She dismissed the internal warnings. Forced them into silence. With time to spare she set off for the party.

★ ★ ★

Since their last meeting, Sanjay had been concerned about Kalindra, but he had no chance to talk to her. Further strangulations occurred. The city was strangely silent, as though holding its breath, waiting for the inevitable. Women feared to travel. Although they worked all hours, the police were still baffled. There were no witnesses. No one heard anything. There was no extraneous D.N.A. *Somebody* must have seen something, heard something. Nobody came forward.

Each murder was committed near an underground station. Women shunned their male colleagues. Refused to work without the presence of other women.

That night an emergency call summoned the police to Upper John Street. They had found a girl, dead. When Sanjay arrived, the forensic team was already examining the victim. He turned to the informants.

'We left the Palladium,' the man said, 'strolled to Piccadilly Circus to take the tube to our hotel at Hyde Park Corner. As we reached Upper John Street, we almost stumbled over the body of this girl.'

The woman beside him was pale, trying to compose herself. The man held his wife close, protectively.

'My wife was screaming,' the man said, 'she got a bit hysterical. Well, it's not something you expect to see, is it? I checked to see if the girl had a pulse. Then called the emergency services. We didn't notice anybody else … we're on our honeymoon you see.'

The fifteenth strangulation! Still nothing. No witnesses. No connections, other than the oval depressions. Even the police were becoming edgy. The less experienced officers were murmuring that it was as if they were fighting an invisible murderer.

Then Sanjay moved across to look at the victim. He stood, unable to move, unable to believe. His whole body shook as Kalindra's vacant eyes stared up at him. His stomach compressed, threatened to send back his last meal. In Hindi, he cursed the evil gods. Cursed the good ones too. How could they take Kalindra from him? How could they let this happen? Her grandfather had assured him that she was special, a chosen one. So why … why hadn't the gods protected her?

He turned away, but could not escape the image, which burned into his memory. The centre of her forehead bore the now familiar oval indentation. He reeled, almost collapsed. Steadied himself against the wall, lowered himself to the ground. Devastated, he remained there, head in hands. Pain sapped his spirit.

Later, he learned that the killer had used the victim's own scarf to strangle her, and left it behind. It was too much for him to bear. Forensic evidence later revealed one confusing piece of evidence. There was no doubt, the trace of silk taken from the first, and subsequent victims, matched Kalindra's scarf. Weighed down by unbearable grief, this information was too much for his shattered mind. His subconscious took over, buried the facts until he would be able to deal with them.

Sanjay took time off work. It was inconceivable that life could be so cruel. If only I had spoken to her again, he thought, ensured she understood. As my wife she would not have been out alone at night. But accepting the guilt did not ease his burden. He knew without doubt that he would never forgive himself, or the gods.

He insisted on being present when they searched Kalindra's house. The thought of strangers touching her belongings, possibly without due respect, was intolerable. Officers paid no attention to the open chest or Hindi scripts. This was not a sectarian killing.

After they left, Sanjay took a closer look. He scanned the foxed manuscripts. They referred to the gods and their many forms, in particular Lord Shiva and his consort, the goddess Kāli. From 1853, his great, great grandfather wrote three of the slender journals. The four other bindings were research by his great grandfather from 1903 onwards.

He settled down to read everything thoroughly. It related to a fanatical sect, of whom he knew little, a sect of Phansigars, assassins, who worshipped their goddess Kāli. She gave her devotees a square cloth, instructing them to strangle victims, mainly travellers. They must offer these human sacrifices to her, their goddess. This method of killing was *thuggee*. The manuscript indicated that his great, great grandfather had been a devout follower, who had offered many sacrifices.

Two sections were heavily marked, the first: "The power of Kāli abides in every woman". The second was more explicit: "A chosen one will bear my name and will be my vessel on earth. My followers will continue the rituals of sacrifice as I decree. If the vessel proves worthy, I will reside in her forever. If not ... she will perish at the hands of my followers."

Sanjay sat back, his hands shook. 'No,' he muttered, 'it is mythological rubbish. There is no foundation in these ancient tales.'

With his hands still shaking, he carefully unfolded the yellowed newspaper clippings. A bold headline stated that the Government museum in Madras had been broken into. Thieves had stolen several smaller artefacts, and desecrated one of the treasures. They had gouged out a red oval stone that had been the central eye of a statuette of Lord Shiva, who is depicted as having three eyes. The sun is his right eye and the moon his left eye; these represent his activity in the physical world. The eye in the centre of his forehead is fire and symbolizes spiritual knowledge and power. It is known as the eye of wisdom or knowledge and, like fire, the powerful gaze of Lord Shiva's third eye annihilates evil. All evildoers feared the third eye.

It was ridiculous, Sanjay thought. Besides, the original victims had all been male travellers. Now every victim was female. But, he wondered, could followers still perform the ancient rites? And why should they now offer female victims? Why would they fear the third eye?

Further newspaper articles bewailed the missing stone, and there was a report that two women had been seen running from the museum on the night of the theft. Many believed that Lord Shiva's consort, the goddess Kāli, would seek retribution, and that death and destruction would follow.

Sanjay reached for the last of the handwritten journals. His ancestor believed that Kāli would wreak a terrible vengeance for the desecration of her Lord Shiva's third eye. If the goddess should ever know of the stone's location, she would combine its wisdom and knowledge with her own evil forces. Every man, or woman, commits some wrongdoing, however slight, so anyone could become her victim. However, if the stone should fall into the hands of a chosen one, that woman would become Kāli's vessel and the goddess's power would be formidable, unspeakable. I believe that should any of this occur, the victims would be mainly female, to atone for the desecration.

Sanjay shuddered. His beloved Kalindra was a chosen one ... those had been her grandfather's very words. But what was the significance of the oval indentations? There was no reference to that in the manuscripts, no indication that it was part of the old rituals. Although, he reasoned, the missing stone was oval. Was it possible? ... His mind drifted towards the desecrated statuette. It seemed that followers believed that the power of Kāli was unimaginable. Was it retribution? He reached for the police box containing Kalindra's effects. Took out her brooch. The oval centre was empty. He shivered. No! It was impossible. Merely coincidence. He checked the list of her belongings: one brooch, centre missing. Perhaps the murderer stole it, or if it was loose it could have fallen out during the attack. Maybe somebody found it, or maybe it rolled into the gutter, down a drain to be lost forever.

Kalindra was the last victim. The killer remained undiscovered. Sanjay said nothing of the chest's contents, he knew his colleagues would ridicule him and it *was* irrelevant.

★ ★ ★

Two years later, whilst on holiday at Southend-on-Sea with her family, a young woman walked along the beach, a silk scarf protected her hair from the sea breeze. She hoped to find attractive shells and pebbles to add to her collection. A red, oval stone caught her attention and she stooped to pick it up. Imakālia cradled the smooth stone, felt its power. It was the most compelling thing she had ever seen. As she gazed at its iridescence beauty, the vibrant reds mesmerised her, swirled towards her, pulled her into their depths. She gasped as the sulphurous intensity of a seething volcano scorched her throat. It then plunged her, shivering, into an icy vermilion maelstrom. It breathed life into her. She knew that they had been awaiting each other.

The mid-day sun emerged from behind a cloud, then, just for an instant, she was staring into the eye of some strange being. She felt as if this stone held her very life and decided that it must always be a part of her. She took it to a jeweller and asked if he could make a pendant to enable her to keep it close to her heart.

Nine days later, the police discovered a woman's body. The murderer had used a silk scarf or cord to strangle her and an oval indentation marked the centre of her forehead.

THE PERFECT CRIME

The Campervan door burst open, Cotter scrambled in, takeaways clutched to his scrawny chest. He turned. Yanked the door shut. Sprung the lock.

Baz frowned. 'You've flattened our dinner.'

'I was cold.' Cotter snivelled, wiped his nose on his sleeve. 'And them village people gave me funny looks. Do you think they're on to us?'

'Nah!' You use this,' Baz said as he tapped the side of his head. 'Nobody saw us when we did that big house over on Tuesday night. We stay here. Pretend we're campers, enjoying the countryside. Same as them caravans we saw last summer.'

'That's right clever,' Cotter said. He grinned foolishly, eyes bright.

Baz puffed out his chest.

Cotter stretched his arms, tried to move his legs. 'How long do you reckon we'll keep this old Campervan? It's doing me back in.' As he manoeuvred, his bony legs and feet overflowed the bench, created a beaver dam in the narrow, debris-strewn aisle.

'Until the heat's off us,' Baz said. 'Shift yer feet!' He squeezed past Cotter's retreating feet, plonked his mass on the larger bunk he'd bagged for himself. 'What's up with it? It was a good deal.' He knew that Cotter wouldn't doubt his judgment. 'I swapped it for that stuff we nicked. Of course, if we stayed here, we could nick a better one, spray it, take the plates off this...'

'Jeez, Baz, I'd rather go back home.'

'I'm only saying, if... but I reckon this next job's going to set us up.'

Cotter leaned forward. Eyebrows raised, eyes wide open. 'Who are we doing over?' His feet tapped excitedly, his head nodded in unison. 'Tell us, Baz. Go on, tell us.'

'This one's a cinch,' Baz said with a splutter. He bowed his shaven head as he shovelled handfuls of fish and chips into his gaping mouth. 'Some old bag. She's loaded.'

With a black-rimmed nail, Cotter scratched his matted red hair, prodded a piece of chicken from his tooth. Then, hand poised for the next mouthful, he said, 'How'd you know she's loaded?'

'Last night... Don't you want that last bit?' Without waiting for a reply, Baz snaffled the remainder of Cotter's meal. Guzzled the food, wiped the residue down his T-shirt and let out a protracted belch. 'Last night,' he said, 'I was chatting up that blonde bit at the Red Lion and these two geezers was whispering about it. They've got it all set up. They're doing her over tomorrow night. We go in tonight. It's perfect.'

A furrow crossed Cotter's freckled brow. 'I don't get it.'

'Don't get what?'

'Why don't they go in tonight?'

Baz revelled in his own superiority. 'Like I said, they haven't a clue. They weren't jobbers. They were right toffs, like in them old movies: "Ah say, old boy".'

'Hey, that were good Baz, *you'd* make a toff.'

'Course I would, all I need's money,' Baz said. 'Well, them two would only do over a class place.'

Cotter's eyes were now full mooned. 'We're going to do a *real* big job then?'

'Not half,' Baz said. 'It just takes brains, like what I've got.' He spread his grubby paws. Each sausage finger, nails bitten to the quick, bore a tattooed letter that spelt out his claim: '*I am the best*'.

'That's right,' Cotter said. 'But you haven't said. How do you know she's loaded?'

'What I heard was she don't use a bank and she's got stacks of jewellery and silver.'

Cotter's bottom lip gaped as he gazed at his hero.

'Do you know where she lives?'

'Course I know where she bloody lives!' Baz sighed, his midriff wobbled with frustration. 'You must have been checking over the getaway car when brains was dished out.'

'I weren't, Baz. Honest.'

Baz shook his head. He'd never admit it, but he needed Cotter. His mate could crank any engine and drove like a demented demon if the law was mentioned. As soon as the lad could squeeze a grease gun, his father, Getaway Gav, had passed on the family trade, but mechanical genius had overloaded Cotter's brain, paralysed his lamppost frame with the simplistic mind of a seven year old. Better get some shuteye, he thought as he pulled his blanket over his clothes and boots.

Later, Cotter's voice shattered his mate's million pound dream robbery. 'Hey, Baz! It's November.'

'You what?'

'It's November,' Cotter repeated.

'I know it's bloody November! Then it'll be December. Get some sleep.'

'You don't get it,' Cotter said. 'You can't go camping in November.'

Baz sat up. '*If* we had a stove. *If* we were camping nuts. We'd go camping in November. Right?'

'But we haven't got no stove,' Cotter said.

'Bloody hell! Do I have to spell it out?' Baz gritted his teeth. '*They* don't know we haven't got a stove, do they?'

Three hours later, Baz woke. Gave Cotter a kick on the shin with his scuffed down-at-heel size elevens. They donned their burglary gear: jeans and black anoraks, with balaclavas perched on their brow, cap style.

Baz shoved a couple of bin bags in Cotter's pocket.

'Got to have something for all that loot. Where's your torch?'

'Under me pillow,' Cotter said, eyes innocent as a child's.

'We're going on a bloody job! How are you going to see where you're going? How you going to find the loot?'

Baz retrieved the torch before they climbed into the cab. At the insistence of his mate, Cotter drove slowly down the eerie country lanes. Trees extended their branches, signposted the way. Hedges whispered incantations. Baz waved him past the deserted house. After a short distance, they parked off the road where overhanging trees wove a shelter and undergrowth conspired towards their concealment.

Baz opened the door allowing the stale stink of their sweat, intermingled with food residue, to drift into the crisp autumn night. They scrambled out. Pulled the balaclavas over their faces. No stars shone a friendly twinkle. Clouds feathered, obscured the moon's crescent. The two men blended with the wind-blown, unknown shapes, like darkened ghosts venturing into a shifting landscape.

'I don't like all these fields and stuff,' Cotter whispered, closing in on Baz.

'Get off!'

Cotter shivered. Edged away an inch or two and looked around. 'It's spooky. There isn't no lights. No pubs. There isn't even a proper path. And what's all them noises?'

'Don't you know nothing? Them's just animals and things,' Baz said.

An owl screeched.

Cotter swivelled his head. Grabbed his mate's arm.

'That weren't no animal, Baz. Somebody's on to us.'

'Pack it in. It were one of them... things. Now, shut your bloody gob.'

In silence, they dogged the hedgerow, crept closer to the house. The windows were tantalising caverns. Guarding the secrets within, neither curtain nor light relieved the emptiness. A gust of wind whipped the gate into a squeaking frenzy, warning fingers of the lower branches pecked at their faces. Cotter dawdled. Baz dug him in the ribs to urge him forward. He hissed threats to prevent his mate from turning back. In a sudden gust of wind, the gate yawned, allowed them access. Close to the hedge, Cotter hesitated, awaited instructions.

'Right,' Baz whispered, 'we stick to the hedge, all the way down. Go slow, and *keep your gob shut.'*

They merged with the shadows, picked their way towards the silent house. Their progress was slow. Cotter kept glancing at the shrubbery as it created animated illusions, but with a threatening glare Baz urged him onwards. The overgrown garden dispatched brambles to spy on their whereabouts, trees heaved up roots to trip clumsy feet. Creepers rampaged, strove to entangle the intruders' arms.

No alarm jangled as they crept under the blind windows, nobody intercepted their approach to the back door.

'Not a sound,' Baz whispered. He grasped the

doorknob. Turned it. There was no resistance as he inched the old, heavy door ajar. No squeak. No creak. Four eyes searched, were reassured. The villains entered, closed the door behind them. Motionless, they listened. Not a sound escaped from the gloom within. A smell of decay hung in the air, colluded with the silence to alleviate their fears. Even the grandfather clock in the hall surveyed them in silence, as its stilled pendulum hung morosely.

Once he was sure of their safety, Baz elbowed Cotter. 'You do upstairs,' he said. 'If there's trouble, you're faster than me. I'll do downstairs.'

'On me own? You didn't say I had to go in on me own.'

'Bloody hell! Get on with it. Sooner we're in, sooner we're out.'

Baz watched Cotter creep towards the staircase. Watched a spear of torchlight echo his mate's stick insect frame as he crossed the gape of the landing window. A turn in the stairs then swallowed him from view.

Alone on the ground floor, Baz worked methodically. He pulled open the first door on his left, his torch revealed mops, brooms and a bucket. With a shrug he closed the door, there were no hiding places in that cupboard.

The second door had no handle. Gingerly, he pushed. It opened onto a platform that flung stone steps down into the abyss. His eyes gleamed with expectancy. Previous cellars had reaped a good harvest.

He stepped onto the platform, nudged the door shut with his elbow. His torch highlighted the steps, showed the way to be uncluttered. Once at the bottom, he scanned the cobweb-strewn walls. There were no shelves, no wooden arms holding treasure.

Disappointed, he shuffled up the steps. Reached for the doorknob. But there was no doorknob. No handle, only a keyhole. He bent down to put his fingers under the gap. There was no gap. He shone his torch along the edges. The door was an exact fit, sides, bottom and top. He crouched, put his eye to the keyhole. Blackness stared back.

'Bloody hell, I can't get out,' he mumbled. He hunkered down on the platform. 'I'll wait for Cotter. He knows I never leave a job without him. He'll find me.'

Ten minutes later, Baz muttered, 'Where the hell's he got to? Stupid bloody idiot.'

He heard a muffled thud. The door inched open.

'Cotter,' he whispered. 'Is that you?'

Baz edged forward. Slid his fingers round the door edge, opened it further. Stuck his head out. Saw nothing. He stepped out. Large hands grabbed his arms, while more hands pressed a cloth against his mouth. His body relaxed. Crumpled to the floor.

★ ★ ★

Baz stirred. Prised one eye open. The familiar surroundings of their Campervan greeted him.

Confused, he sat up, saw Cotter, sprawled at his side, snoring. Baz dug his mate in the ribs.

'Wazzup! It weren't me, honest,' Cotter said. 'I haven't done nothing.'

'Wake up!'

'You said that place were empty, except for that old bird,' Cotter said. 'Somebody nearly did for me. They pounced on me and shoved some rag in my mouth. It had a nice taste though, like sweets. What happened?'

'I don't know,' Baz said. 'I can't remember anything after I came out of that cellar.'

The two stood up, checked their various limbs were complete, and in working condition.

'I didn't like being on me own,' Cotter said, 'there was cobwebs and spiders, *and* the floorboards creaked. It was spooky.'

'Stop moaning,' Baz said. Then he peered through the grimy window. 'Bloody hell! Somebody's moved our van. With us in it!'

Cotter looked out of the opposite window. 'M1 Motorway.'

'You what!'

'M1 Motorway,' Cotter said, 'that's what the signpost says. M1 Motorway - South, and it points to that road on the left.'

Baz rushed to the window. 'We've been rumbled. That village has kicked us out – set us on our way home.' He dived towards the hidey-hole under his bunk. Gasped in relief. 'Our stash is safe. *And* the stuff we nicked on the way up here.'

Cotter peered over his shoulder. 'That gear from Tuesday's haul has gone!'

'Bloody hell,' Baz said, 'we *have* been done over. Those villagers have nicked back all the gear we took from that big house in the village. But they haven't touched the other stuff. Maybe there is honour among thieves.'

'So do you think they're on to us?' Cotter's brow furrowed. 'Shall we carry on pretending we're camping?'

'Shurrup,' Baz said, his ego shredded, 'and drive.'

NOCTURNE IN E FLAT

Tendrils of the industrial grape vine spread the news of Geoffrey Gruber's demise. Hoover's neck hairs bristled, a sudden chill made him shudder. Yet another death. Then he shrugged. It was to be expected. Gruber, a fifty-eight year old contemporary, was a weak-willed nobody, whose passing would cause no more than a slight ripple in the commercial world. Only like-minded simpletons would mourn him, simple men who believed in the importance of courtesy, compassion and co-operation. Those who sought achievement in the business world did not advance by kindly gestures and a generous nature. He was proud of his analytical approach, proud of his lack of sentimentality and firmly believed that a good kick in the teeth, figuratively of course, always achieved the desired results and subservience.

His memories of Gruber were all negative. Firstly, the man was slow-minded, easy to manipulate, a man destined to a life in the lower echelons of the business world. But he was also a smoker of cheap acrid cigars. Only when Gruber kept a reasonable distance, was he bearable from an olfactory point of view. However once he came within range, his gin-breath and body odour competed with the acrid smoke to sour any man's stomach. The man was obviously unaware of the discovery of mouthwashes and deodorants, even strong mints seemed to be beyond his reach. Hoover, having decided his character assassination was complete, then dismissed Gruber from his mind.

After handling the particularly difficult take-over of a lucrative company, Hoover walked the short distance to his club. He liked the tranquillity, rather like a car wash brushes away the grime of the day, so the club swept away the day's dirty-dealings, cleansing him for life at home. A turkey sandwich on wholemeal bread satisfied his hunger, a tonic water quenched his thirst. He relaxed, contented ... and not a cheap cigar within smelling distance.

He drove home, parked the car and clicked the self-lock. The silence surprised him. It was that quiet time between work and leisure, but there were usually *some* people about. Peering round the dimly lit underground car park, he saw that the area was deserted. Muffled footsteps crept behind him. He turned sharply. Saw nothing. But he was rarely wrong, his senses were finely tuned and he was certain somebody was lurking in the shadows. He hesitated. Then laughed at this momentary weakness. It was a short walk to the elevator, which would take him to his penthouse apartment, and, should some ruffian decide to tackle him, his efforts would be futile. Hoover flexed his muscles, stretched to his full six foot three inches. He believed that a healthy body fostered a healthy mind and he was fit from regular workouts in his home gym. Even in his business suit it would be clear to anyone that he had a well-toned body. It would take a brave, and foolish, fellow to take him on.

Again, he looked swiftly round before stepping into the elevator. He pressed the button. For the second time that day, his neck hairs bristled, caused him to take an involuntary step back. The elevator slid to a halt on the top floor. *His* top floor. No other apartment shared this prime position. There were four lower apartments, but his was "E" ... for excellence naturally. His hand was poised, key at the ready, but he heard another's breathing beside his own, felt a warm breath on his neck. He spun round. No other person stood on the small bare landing. He unlocked the door, slid inside, turned the key in the deadlock and threw the bolts at top and bottom. A businessman always has enemies, he thought, but he was prepared. No assailant would get the better of him.

A glass of single malt relaxed his body and mind. Another allowed him to forget the earlier flashes of uncertainty. He needed an early night. His workload had been heavy recently and his body felt sleep deprived. He undressed, showered and towelled his hair dry. Pyjama clad, he padded into the sitting room. Switched off the light. The view to the north, away from the city's light-pollution, was relaxing. He knew nothing of astronomy, but a boyhood memory had stayed with him. It was a clear night. Visibility was excellent allowing Ursa Major to dominate the sky and there, within it, was the distinctive outline of the Plough. It felt like his own private canvass, painted by a minimalist artist, framed by his sitting room window.

Someday, he thought, after retiring, he would maybe buy a telescope, study astronomy. That feeling of permanence in the heavens both encouraged and comforted him. The first man ever to start trading had looked at those same stars, possibly gained inspiration from them. Once successful, maybe that ancient businessman had then relaxed under their protection.

Hoover yawned. Left the curtains drawn back. Then he rechecked the locks and bolts on his door. His bedroom overlooked the edge of the city. He glanced down. Shrugged. Far below the minions crawled, ant-like. He had no time for their meaningless lives, their petty aspirations. Lights flashed. Traffic sped by. The city was coming to life again. As was his custom, he left the large window bare so that nothing stood between him and the sky. He liked to lie in bed, allow the stars, and in its cycle, the moon, to shed a tranquil light that relaxed him, prepared him for a well-deserved night's sleep. He flopped onto the crisp sheet. Pulled the duvet over his shoulders and settled down on his left side.

A sudden pressure on his right shoulder disturbed his sleep. He snapped on the light. Since nothing stirred within the room, he assumed that he had been dreaming and flicked the room into darkness. With no further distraction he wrapped the duvet round his shoulders once more. Again he awaked with a start. Somebody, or at least something, was resting on his shoulder. By now the full moon had risen in the sky. It shone directly onto his bed. His large wardrobe occupied the wall adjacent to his bed, suitably positioned for its mirror to reflect his own image. He looked. Nothing perched on his bed. Nothing rested on his shoulder.

Hoover switched on the light. Sat up. Looked round. Everything was as it should be, as it always was. He concluded that he had been restless and his struggles had resulted in the duvet pulling tightly against his shoulder. Once more, he settled down, but for the most part, sleep eluded him.

He awoke at five-thirty with the duvet wedged under his body and trapped around his feet. It was Saturday, ought to have been his day for a lie-in. With the distractions of the previous evening and night forgotten, he went straight to his gym, performed his usual exercises and weight training. Afterwards the shower cleansed his sweating body. He stood for some minutes, allowed the water to ripple over his muscles, cascade down his strong legs. It felt good.

His stomach rumbled, encouraged him to think of breakfast. It was still early, but with only himself to please, he reasoned that time was immaterial. A large glass of pure orange juice accompanied two poached eggs on toasted wholemeal bread. It smelt good. Tasted better. As the coffee percolated, he looked forward to a leisurely day. He switched on the news.

'... *Geoffrey Gruber, who died yesterday, will be sadly...*'

Hoover snapped off the radio. Sunk back into his chair as the memory of the previous day came rushing over him. It took him by surprise, he wasn't one to dwell on the past, or on anyone's demise let alone some loser like Gruber. The day had started badly. He contemplated returning to bed to compensate for lost sleep. Decided against it. At least he could expect a good sleep during the coming night.

The lift pinged its arrival. His letterbox clattered. Then the lift descended, left him in peace. He collected his daily paper from the doormat. Full of anticipation, he turned the pages. Naturally, he already knew that the honour was his, but to see it confirmed in print was exhilarating. And there it was. He grinned. His name stood proudly among the New Year's Honours List.

He tried it out for size: 'Sir Hoover Robinson. *Sir* Hoover Robinson.' Carefully, he cut out the page. It would join the scrapbook that detailed his advancements. Time had proved his superiority and now the ultimate accolade; the Queen would bestow the knighthood upon him in recognition of his business acumen.

The same edition of his newspaper reaffirmed the death of Geoffrey Gruber. That earlier cloud reappeared to darken his jubilation. Hoover shivered.

This was the fourth death in as many weeks, although quite unremarkable one would suppose, given their age. However the striking thing was that Hoover had known all four in his earlier days. More than known them. They were among the many whose hands he had mangled during his climb to the top of the business ladder. That old saw about being pleasant to people as one climbed up the ladder, because one would inevitably meet them on the way down made him laugh. There wasn't a chance that he would be meeting anybody because he did not intend to descend that particular ladder. He was safe. His innate quest for privacy had kept his shady dealings under wraps, away from ferreting journalists, out of sight of jealous rivals.

All day, having forgotten his earlier resolve to pass the day in idleness, he busied himself with household tasks. Keeping occupied allowed no time for ridiculous feelings to emerge. He prepared a curry for dinner, took delight in slicing and dicing, it reminded him of former rivals, encouraged him to keep a sharp edge against any up and coming competitors, stupid snappy pups who thought they could out-manoeuvre the master.

After his evening meal, he chose, at random, a DVD from his collection. But before the film had even begun, Hoover heard a slight tap at his door. That was strange, he thought, the lift's blip always announced the imminent arrival of visitors. Nobody was invited to his door, and he soon sent the uninvited scurrying.

Nobody ever gained admittance. Determined to dismiss his would-be guest as quickly as possible, he opened the door. The landing was empty. And, even though he hadn't heard the lift's descent, the light indicated that it waited silently on the garage level. The locks on the stairway door stood firm, nobody had arrived or left from that direction. He shook his head. It wasn't in his nature to image things, but he concluded that he must have been mistaken. He closed the door. Turned the deadlock and drew the bolts. Put the key in his pocket. A low voice came from his sitting room.

He marched in, temper flaring. Cursing and swearing, he imagined what he would do to various parts of the intruder's anatomy. But the sitting room was empty, even the DVD was still in silent mode. Knowing that nobody could leave the apartment without the key to the deadlock, he started his search. He checked everywhere: in each cupboard and wardrobe, under the bed, even inside the kitchen units, dishwasher and washing machine. Nothing!

No longer in the mood for a film, he ejected the DVD and returned it to its case. Perhaps a little Chopin would settle these newfound nerves. He took the bottle of malt and a tumbler over to the sofa, sank into its welcoming comfort. But even his favourite nocturne didn't have the same sensuously fluctuating harmony. In fact it seemed almost discordant. Perhaps an early night would serve him well.

He turned on his left side, tucked the duvet around his shoulders and, with closed eyes, he tried to relax. A hand rested on his shoulder. Yes, he was sure it was a hand. It seemed to press its fingers into his flesh. He looked in the mirror. Although the room was gloomy, the shadows long, he could clearly see that no one rested on his bed. No hand accosted his shoulder.

He turned his head slightly to watch the stars shine from their appointed place like stepping-stones across a heavenly sea. Such tranquillity was calming, however, before they could influence his mood, he heard his front door open and close. His stomach lurched. His anger erupted. He leapt out of bed. Raced along the hallway. Then stopped abruptly. The security locks and bolts still guarded his front door. In frustration, he thumped the door as if it were the culprit. Then he checked through the whole apartment. All the while he cursed the intruder, mumbled and cursed what he would do to the villain when he found him. But, once again, nobody was there.

He clenched his fists, furious with himself. 'Of course there isn't anybody here! How could there be,' he muttered. 'No other person has a key.'

Hoover's previous lack of sleep crept up on him, allowed his rage to subside. He returned to bed. Again, his sleep was disturbed. He heard the door to the sitting room open. With absolute certainty, he knew that nobody was there, so he took a different tack. He counted the seconds. Intrigued, he waited. Held his breath. There was only one place for the intruder to go, the gym and its integral bathroom could hold no interest. He tugged down the duvet so that he had a clear view of his bedroom door. He watched. Waited. Waited for the doorknob to turn. With his lungs almost at bursting point, he slowly released the de-oxygenated air. All else was silent. The doorknob did not turn.

He clicked on the bedside light, reached across the double bed to light its twin. Then he padded along the floor and switched on the overhead light. He opened the en suite door, illuminated its interior. Deciding that he could afford no more distractions, that he *must* sleep, he cautiously opened the bedroom door. Light flooded into the small hallway. Already he felt calmer. He closed the sitting room curtains. Switched on every light in his apartment, left all the doors ajar. Then he put his favourite nocturne on the CD player. Set "repeat" and turned up the sound. He retreated to his bedroom. With Chopin's Nocturne in E Flat Major overriding any sounds and the lights deterring intruders, he settled down, sure he would sleep soundly. It was not to be. Something, somebody, intended to keep him awake.

His sleep was shattered when a strong hand clasped his shoulder. Immediately, he looked in the mirror. No hand clasped his shoulder, no weight pressed down. Desperate for sleep, he determined that whatever happened it would not disturb him and resolved to deal with it in the morning. He stacked all the pillows against his bed-head and then sank his back and head against them. Sleep's cradle refused to comfort him. No sleep-dust settled in his eyes. His thoughts tussled with the mystery of the unknown intruder. He *knew* that somebody was there, or at least had been there. But how was that possible? That was the question. How? He'd bought the apartment off-plan, had all his own modifications installed. There were no hidden passageways, no secret compartments. Before moving in, he had a full-height gate installed at the top of the staircase. Trusting no one, he immediately bought an identical lock for both that and his front door and replaced them himself. His privacy was sacrosanct.

It was puzzling. Annoying. How could somebody gain access to his apartment without his knowledge? The roof was a possibility, although he kept his double glazed windows securely locked. What about the floor below? But anyone attempting that climb, if indeed such a climb was possible, would have the same problem. That is, there was no entry from outside. There was only one possibility. And that possibility shook him to the core. He didn't believe in such things, never had. But there was no getting away from it ... he was being haunted. And of one thing he felt certain: dead or alive, Gruber was at the bottom of it. It was undoubtedly him and his cronies. They were here for revenge. Not that it was justified mind. He had dealt hard, but fair ... most of the time ... well some of the time, he conceded. Damn it all! All's fair in business, isn't it?

The next morning, Sunday, he slept late. It was already past noon when he awoke. He showered and dressed. Feeling rather stupid, he flicked off all the lights. Then, in a fit of bravado, he opened one of the long, but shallow top windows in his bedroom. The place needed a little airing. He fetched the Sunday papers from the doormat, dropped them on the sofa. His stomach was tense not wanting food, but he made an omelette, which he took together with his coffee through to the sitting room.

The business section, always his first port of call, announced the death of yet another city man. He threw the paper down in disgust.

He didn't want to know who had died. Didn't want to know if it was another of his rivals. Another rival come to join the fray. They were amassing for an attack, and he was the target. Well they wouldn't win. They didn't win before and they wouldn't now. He would show them. Daylight was receding and for the remainder of the afternoon, after once again switching on all the lights, he tried to decide how to rid himself of this phantom intruder. Although not a churchgoer, he considered asking a priest to perform an exorcism in his apartment, to cleanse the place. Another thought was to call in one of those ghost-busting teams that he had heard about. Then he immediately wondered if that was all TV hoo-ha. He managed a weak laugh at the thought of a group of sane adults chasing ghosts. The laugh froze on his face. *He* had a ... well ... without a doubt he had something. And he needed either explanation or extermination. Preferably both.

A clap of thunder distracted him, lightning following within six seconds. Even through the double-glazing, he could hear the wind howling. There was a sudden pounding and the howling intensified. He ran to the bedroom. The catch holding the top window had unhooked. Repeatedly, the window yawned in the gale, then snapped shut. With other things on his mind, he had forgotten to close and relock it. He grasped the handle, yanked it, but his hands couldn't fight the wind's strength. Pulling a chair over, he climbed up and tried to force the window shut, to no avail. He peered at the frame, checked all round the window. There was no extraneous material. Yet *something* caused an obstruction. No matter how much force he used, the window refused to fully close. He compromised. Closed the handle on its second notch and turned the key. After all, the gap was less than two inches wide, far too small for anyone to gain admission. And it was securely locked, even though the gale force wind whistled and whined through the narrow gap. He was satisfied that nothing else could enter. Nothing physical, that is.

The storm was strengthening, the sky showed no sign of it letting up. The lights flickered. His brow furrowed with fear as he remembered his childhood fear of darkness, a childhood horror that seemed to be reasserting itself. He would be prepared, just in case. The kitchen cupboard revealed his torch, with batteries charged. Then he hunted round for candles. All he could find was a box with half-a-dozen tea lights and a single two-inch diameter candle. They would have to do. But he prayed that the lights wouldn't fail. He prayed as he had never prayed before and for several hours, much to his relief, the electricity remained connected.

During the early evening, as he settled on the sofa, he contemplated having another early night. The lights flickered again. He frowned. His stomach gnawed at him as the earlier concerns resurfaced. Almost ready to get down on his knees in supplication, he glanced again at the clock: eight thirty two. Scarcely a minute later, his apartment was plunged into total darkness. Even the Plough had succumbed to the storm and could only continue furrowing the sky in secrecy. His window frame now merely enclosed darkness after meteorological thieves had stolen his heavenly painting.

He decided that his only option was to retire to bed. Neither Chopin nor the array of lights could accompany him that night. Even the moon had fled in fright, scuttled into shelter. The storm was so intense it excluded, it seemed to him, the whole universe. In the pitiful light from the candles he undressed. Then he remembered he had a bottle of sleeping pills left over from an earlier episode of sleeplessness some two or three years past. He rummaged in the bathroom cabinet. Found his treasure. Only two left. He swallowed them both. Glared at his mirror image. A strangely gaunt image returned his stare. Hoover recoiled. It seemed that this situation *was* affecting him more than he realised. Well, he thought, they can do their worst now. I shall sleep through it all.

He curled up on his left side, pulled the duvet round his shoulders. The sleeping tablets were slow acting. His mind wandered, but common sense told him that there were no such things as ghosts; they were merely the ramblings of people with an over-imaginative mind. And he certainly didn't have an imagination, let alone a vivid one. Unless making money was involved. Yet... There was no other explanation. No logical reason for the events that had occurred. Something was definitely walking through his apartment, trifling with him. Taunting him. He became drowsy, hardly aware of his surroundings. Only rain lashing the windows and the incessant howling of the wind, kept him from sleep. Again, he cursed the top window, if it wasn't for that, he would be asleep by now. Eventually, exhaustion won the battle. He slept.

An explosive thunderclap disturbed him. Drum rolls of rain pounded the windows, the angry wind growled and howled through the window's crevice.

Again, he cursed the window. Now, fully awake, he knew he would have a restless night. But something distracted him. He smelled burning. Smoke drifted towards his nostrils. He coughed as the acrid fumes threatened his throat.

'Gruber!'

It *was* Gruber. He'd know that overpowering cheap cigar anywhere. The candle flickered and guttered in the draft. The tea lights gave sparse light but left great corners of the room in total darkness. He knew with absolute certainty that it was Gruber. Of course, he reasoned, as Gruber died on Friday, this ... this thing in his apartment could not be him. A faint smell came closer. At first, he couldn't place it, not until, that is, it was upon him. His stomach almost retched as he tasted the stink of Gruber's gin-breath mixed with his body odour.

Hoover tried analysing the situation. Gruber, along with any business associates knew that he abhorred smoking. They would also have known that to any lover of single malts, the second-hand smell of gin would be repellent. Hoover had proved conclusively that it was impossible for any living person to be in that apartment. And, as Gruber was most certainly dead, then logic decreed that only one possibility remained – however improbable – Gruber's ghost was haunting him. And the rat was making sure that Hoover knew the identity of his tormenter. Having his suspicions confirmed did nothing to alleviate Hoover's peace of mind. For one thing, how does one deal with a ghost?

The wind crying through the crevice caught his attention. No! It wasn't the wind. It was a voice. Gruber's voice. 'Hoooover, Hoooover.'

He cursed Gruber with all the profanities known to man, cursed with such strength of feeling that, dead or alive, any man would quake in perpetual damnation.

The tea lights flickered for the last time. Left him in total darkness. A hand clamped on Hoover's right hand. Another hand clasped the top of his head and forced him down the bed. He gasped for air. Then he felt the full weight of a body spread-eagled over him. He tried to move. Terror held him in its grip. Not a muscle could he move. His breathing became irregular. Each time he let out a breath, the weight from above filled the space before he could inhale another gulp of air. He took swift, shallow breaths. But his assailant was quicker and his weight pressed Hoover further into the mattress. The duvet tightened about him. It enveloped him in a deadly dance.

Mustering together all his strength, all his resolve, Hoover parried the next attack and retaliated. He was free! He leapt out of bed. In two or three bounds he reached the bedroom door. He wrenched it open. His breathing was erratic, his heart thumping. Then he saw that the bolts were not secured across his front door. He ran forward. The door swayed open to meet him. Confusion ate at his logical thinking. Terror gripped him. He *never* left the door unlocked. Never!

He heard a voice behind him. 'Hooover, Hooover,' it called.

He shuddered. Jumped forward. The lift wasn't at his floor. Then he saw that the gate across the stairs, the gate that he kept permanently locked, was swinging on its hinges. Without stopping to reason, he fled down the stairs. Down and round, down and round his feet pattered on the stone steps. Safely at the bottom, he fought for air. His chest wheezed and croaked in an unaccustomed manner. Hoover felt for his car keys. Nothing! He looked down. Only then did he realise that he was bare-footed and sporting only his silk pyjamas. At that moment, the lift pinged. It was leaving the top floor, his floor. He stared. His feet were leaden, glued to the floor. He gasped in large gulps of air. His lungs expanded. A wave of heat swept up his body and face. Then, cheap, acrid cigar fumes mingled with gin and sweat accosted his nose. The spell was broken, his feet free. He expelled the accumulated air in one long piercing scream as he ran into the night.

MONEY TO BURN

Oliver's first taste of money, real money, was when his father rewarded him with a pound for his efforts in cleaning the family car. This was before decimalisation, before a neat golden coin replaced the rectangle of paper. His pound note was crisp, clean and had a smell he'd never experienced before. He held it by the two bottom corners, studied its engravings.

His two older sisters startled him, their eyes wide and gleaming.

'Let's go down to the sweet shop,' said one.

Oliver gripped the corners. 'I'm not going to *spend* it.'

No sooner had he spoken than the other sister snatched at the note. They ran off, left the ten-year-old boy clutching two tiny scraps of paper. Grief and loss reflected in the remains. It was like losing a friend, or relative, with nothing left to bury. He knew he couldn't say anything. It was their word against his, and his mother always believed the girls, his father, too, when they batted their eyelashes with feminine innocence.

He went to his room. Sat on the edge of the bed, not by choice, simply because there was nowhere else to sit. His parents called his room the box-room. Which was appropriate since there was no room for a conventional bed. After he outgrew his cot, he slept on a camp bed. Behind the door was a space two feet wide, with not an inch to spare on the opening edge. Mother told him not to worry because his father was handy. Oliver sneaked a glance at his father's hands, thought they looked pretty normal, but decided he would keep an eye out to be on the safe side.

He had stood on the landing, kept poking his head round the door to see what was happening. Fascinated, he watched as his father stood two sturdy supports at each end of the room. Then he placed two more in the middle and topped the lot with a length of thick wood. Father screwed the top to the supports. Oliver beamed. It was beginning to look like a bed, a proper bed. On top of this Father placed a mattress, a palliasse so they told him. Straw filled the tough ticking, and, after the rickety camp bed, he found it to be very comfortable. So much so that he had no wish to sleep on an ordinary mattress.

Underneath this contraption was his hidey-hole. A place, where through the years he had stored his toys and treasures. And this, he decided, was where he would secrete any future earnings. But he needed a deterrent, something to keep his sisters out. Because he vowed they would never take any money from him again. He started a collection of bugs. A large spider, rescued when his sisters came screaming from the bathroom, joined the array of beetles, millipedes, and worms. Even at that early age, he recognised that they were terrified of any creature with more than four legs, and equally scared of the legless. He grinned. Realised they weren't too happy about four-legged creatures either.

His plan worked to perfection and he continued to scheme and plot ways of hiding and diverting attention from his money. He had been a quiet child. Quiet and secretive. Unbeknown to his parents, he saved his pocket money, coin by coin and secreted them, in an unused DVD case, under his bed, fronted by an assortment of tubs and boxes marked "Bugs". Even his mother would not venture under there.

But the love, and loss, of that first pound note engraved itself in his memory and each time somebody sent him on an errand he substituted his coins for their paper money. He didn't buy sweets, or comics or anything else. Except for his growing wealth, everything else he possessed had been a birthday or Xmas present, or passed on, second-hand. Day after day, night after night, he checked his growing hoard ... and counted it.

It came as no surprise, at least not to Oliver, that he should excel at maths. All that counting of his secret hoard had stood him in good stead. His parents, however, although very proud, were quite mystified regarding their son's seeming genius, since neither of them could successfully master anything beyond elementary addition. It was, he reflected, fortuitous that they stopped at three, regarding their children that is, for there was no space for a fourth child, of either sex. His sisters spent their sleeping hours on two storeys; their bedroom had only sufficient space for bunk beds.

When the time came, his thoughts did wander towards girls, but although they drew his curiosity, excited him, he never asked them out. He couldn't! It would mean spending money. And still his parents didn't know about his obsession. He let them continue to assume that he was studious, a loner with no interest in possessions.

It seemed natural to Oliver that he should apply for a position in a bank. All that wonderful money drew him in like a tractor pulling in a single bale of hay. The interview went well. They were suitable impressed with his exceptional numeracy skills, astounded at his quick grasp of financial matters. He started immediately.

His first task, though not a normal duty of bank tellers, was to slip a blank bankbook into his pocket. He had a plan and the official covers of that bankbook were essential. Oliver was delighted both with his job and his cleverness. However, he soon discovered that his delight was ill founded. Since he kept his own collection hidden in his bedroom, he had never ventured inside a bank. His parents weren't great savers. Both of his sisters were working, but he knew the thought of saving money was beyond their comprehension. They would giggle over their earnings, then giggle some more over their purchases. All that giggling couldn't be good for anyone, he thought.

The first shock came when the bank gave Oliver details of his new account into which they would pay his salary. He hadn't counted on that. It was a bad start to the day, and, to make matters worse, within the first five minutes, a customer demanded to *withdraw* money. He couldn't believe it. The man actually wanted to take money out ... to spend! It was beyond Oliver's comprehension. He felt the colour drain from his face. His hands sweated. His body shook. He knew that he could not complete the transaction. Knew that he was incapable of giving money away! And it didn't matter that the man clearly had a right to his money. At that time, the money was in the bank, and it was his duty, as he saw it, to safeguard the bank's money. Besides, handing over money was alien to everything he believed in.

His breathing became heavy and erratic. He could feel his heart thumping, its pattern was irregular and spasmodic and it caused a severe pain in his chest. Sweat dampened his entire body, caused his hands to become slippery. His arms were in the grip of paralysis. Another employee had to take over. They half dragged, half carried Oliver from his position at the counter and called an ambulance. With the sirens warbling, the ambulance raced to the hospital while the medic kept checking Oliver's condition.

By the time they arrived, his vital signs were almost back to normal. The suspected heart attack was just a memory. It was put down to an exaggerated panic attack, but they kept him in for a few hours, monitored him.

It gave him time to think. Time to realise that, under no circumstances could he continue working at the bank. In fact, now that he knew the full nature of their work, he realised that he would suffer considerable difficulty in walking past a bank. He may even have to resort to crossing over the road since he was fully convinced that his legs were incapable of carrying his body past such a disreputable establishment.

As soon as the hospital discharged him, he gave the bank notice to quit, active immediately. Then he took his time finding more suitable employment. He considered management training for a large supermarket. They had the right idea; they *made* money! Then he remembered that as a future manager he may be responsible for paying out too, presumably the staff were paid wages!

And wages, salaries, whatever, proved to be another problem. Most employers transferred funds directly into the individual's bank account. That wouldn't do. Allow somebody else to hold his money! Never!

While he puzzled over this predicament, he played his trump card. He allowed his sisters to "accidentally" see his bankbook. Inside, he was buzzing with excitement, now that he had ensured that they knew his money was beyond their reach. But the bugs remained ... just in case.

After consideration and elimination, the solution became clear, there was only one thing for it ... he would have to become self-employed. But in what capacity? That was the problem. It would have to be something that required no, or at least very little, outlay. He puzzled long and hard, rejected one thing after another until ... he noticed his mother cleaning the windows. That was it! It was perfect, at least for a start. He could use one of his mother's buckets, her sponge and chamois. To complete his needs, he borrowed his dad's lightweight aluminium ladder that was gathering dust at the back of the garage.

Full of enthusiasm, he walked the neighbourhood in search of customers. He had realised that the normal route was to advertise, but that cost money. After a few weeks, he was washing the windows of about fifty per cent of the properties within walking distance. What's more, they paid in cash. He was delighted. But the more work he carried out, the more money he received acted like a drug. Earning money became an obsession. He wanted more and soon extended his services to include car washing. Then dog washing, which went surprisingly well. Except when some over-enthusiastic pooch took a nip at him. But the embarrassed owner paid him off, in cash.

He continued to live at home, with his parents. He

went out to work. Ate his dinner and then went to his room, ostensibly to study. In fact, the daily ritual of checking and counting his money was his pastime, his entertainment and his passion.

Even after his sisters both married and moved out, he stuck to the imagined interest in bugs. His collection continued to grow ... his collection of the paper stuff, that is. It had long since outgrown the DVD box, outgrown a shoebox. The shoes had been a birthday present, as were most of his clothes since his family never knew what to buy him. What's more, he remained in his own room, refused the luxury of a "proper" bed. He had become inseparable from his straw mattress. It was his symbol of stability, just as money was life.

Later, when his parents bought replacement luggage for their holidays, he claimed an old suitcase. It was just what he needed. Of course, he did not go on vacation with his parents, although they did ask, tried to insist. But he was adamant. He needed to be with his collection. His mother, and sisters, were still revolted by what they thought was his growing collection of bugs.

Every evening, he opened the suitcase. Breathed in the lovely smell of paper money. As a variation to his usual counting procedure, he would sometimes divide the notes into different categories. Usually, this meant division into categories of smell. Although each denomination had its own particular feel and smell, there was something else. He came to recognise where notes had been, who had handled them, at least the employment of the handler.

New notes, straight from the bank, were his favourite. Although they had no extraneous smells, they had an untouched, unsullied feel and a whiff of their own. He kept these in the shoebox within his suitcase, marked out as special so as to remain uncontaminated. He recorded every banknote's serial number in one of his exercise books, along with its own peculiar aroma.

Although he didn't realise it, his "nose" for paper money was akin to that of the best perfumiers or the top wine connoisseurs. But he cared nothing for perfume, even less for wine. What did he want with the first, to sprinkle it about, or the second, to pour it down his throat? He couldn't hold perfume or wine in his fingers, couldn't caress them. How could you hold a liquid in your hands, nuzzle it round your face? He knew the denomination of any bank note simply by holding it.

And so his obsession grew. He wanted, needed money. He needed to collect, to keep collecting without any thought of ever spending what he had. In fact he begrudged the spending of every single penny, even for food.

Each day, his mother prepared a packed lunch, which after a morning's hard work, he ate in the park. It was surprising what people discarded, but it was mostly newspapers. He found the broadsheets more interesting than his father's red tops, and, although there was no prior arrangement, he went to the same seat, at the same time, every day. And was rewarded with an almost pristine copy of *The Times,* which its purchaser regularly discarded in the bin adjacent to the park bench. Thus mentally and bodily recharged, he would walk from one to another of his afternoon appointments.

His mother always had dinner ready for him. So, although his mind was elsewhere, he was obliged to eat his meal. Then he trotted straight upstairs. First, he counted the day's takings. He would rub his hands in satisfaction. Then he wrote down each serial number before sorting the paper money. He stored the coins in a separate box. His interest in them had waned. Because of this, he always handed over coins when paying his mother something towards his keep, which he paid with a smile, although inwardly grudging every penny. It wouldn't do to upset her, to chance that she may suggest he find somewhere else to live. Think of all the rent and other expenses!

All went well. Then one particular day he picked up *The Times.* Saw that one of their journalists had compiled a list of the country's richest people. This list was fascinating, at least until his eyes strayed to the right hand column. The newspaper had included the estimated wealth of each individual. Oliver was distraught. Even the people at the bottom of the list made his collection look pitiful. But what could he do? How could he increase his wealth to match theirs? And even that would not be good enough. He *must* surpass them. Several thoughts entered his mind. Maybe he could win on the lottery, but that would mean actually *buying* a ticket. No, the odds were too great. What about robbing a bank? He could end up locked away, at her Majesty's pleasure, but without her currency. Marry an heiress? That would involve spending money on her first, so that wouldn't do either. Try as he might, no sane, or acceptable, idea presented itself.

A downhearted Oliver completed the afternoon's work. Even after dinner, the counting of his takings did little to improve his melancholy. For several weeks, he worked like an automaton. The only thing that kept him going was the realisation that if he didn't work there would be no money. But the newspaper benefactor unwittingly lifted Oliver's mood, just as he had shattered it previously.

There was a large section dealing with stocks and shares, another devoted to property, particularly buy-to-let. And Oliver realised that those so-called millionaires, even the billionaires didn't have much *actual* money. That is, they didn't have it there to count, to classify, to smell and enjoy. Instead, they tied their money up in bonds, stocks and shares ... along with property development and business investments. *They* couldn't put their hand on good old reliable paper money. Oliver laughed. *Their* money was only *on* paper. So, he decided that, although all the readers thought they knew the secrets of the wealthy, they didn't. They were no wiser. The journalist had duped them. Because he, Oliver, was the richest person ... although, he conceded, he still wanted more.

With this in mind, he continued his work, continued his hoarding of the different notes. Windows, cars and dogs all needed regular cleaning, but it was still not enough. Other entrepreneurs would expand, take on staff, or so he'd heard. Was expansion the answer? There was a snag, a major snag. Employees would expect payment. Even the thought of paying some other person sent his heart racing in protest. He would expand, alone, regardless of the extra hours involved. But what else needed regular cleaning? The wheelie bins that had sprouted in everyone's garden were his first thought, what's more each household had three. His customer list grew, along with a far cleaner neighbourhood. He began to receive requests. Could you clean my paintwork? The budgie/canary/parrot's cage? Then hamsters and guinea pigs joined in. He never refused a request, never refused the extra money.

Then both of his parents died within a short time of each other. According to the latest will, Oliver, unmarried, would remain in the house and only on his death would the house pass to the two sisters, or their offspring. Now he had the choice of either his parents' or his sisters' bedroom, but he still chose to sleep in his cosy box room, upon his unique bed.

His days became longer, his evenings shorter, but there was always time to smell, count and sort his banknotes. All this time it never occurred to him to spend any money. It had never been necessary, except for basic foods and demanding utility bills. Even with these, he refused to use electricity for warmth. Where was the need? The jumble sales were always a good source of extras jumpers.

Then an advertisement regarding funeral expenses drew his attention. It had previously never occurred to him what would happen when he was dead and gone. The old adage about not taking it with you worried him. It niggled and gnarled, and nipped and chewed. His work was beginning to suffer. At the back of his mind, choose whether he was working, receiving money or counting it, the worry remained.

The years had passed, he was over retirement age and still anxious about his collection. The smell of money still intoxicated him. The feel, even in his now gnarled hands, was still the most wonderful sensation. Then he had an idea. He would beat the system. Show the gainsayers that *he* could do it. He would take it with him on his final journey.

He made a will, gave specific instructions about his funeral arrangements. Then he continued as normal, with one exception. He slit the side of his mattress, took out all the straw, disposed of it bundle by bundle in the "green" bin. Then with care, almost reverence, he stacked his collection in neat piles inside the mattress ticking. He re-stitched the gaping hole in a manner that any seamstress that claimed to achieve invisible mending would be proud. Such was the precision of his handiwork that, from the feel of the mattress, nobody would guess its contents.

When his earthly time ended, he knew that his sisters would follow his instructions so as to gain access to his amassed fortune.

And so, in due course, in strict accordance with his wishes, they instructed that he be cremated, together with, and resting upon, the beloved palliasse that had been his since childhood.

GOOD HAUNTING

The ghostmaster general's instructions were explicit: 'Locate the client, haunt his tormentor, give him a taste of his own nastiness'. Even an apprentice ghost could easily trace his client. It was all down to cosmic vibrations. That was the trouble. Several times, Mervin had followed false trails due to distorted vibrations.

He stopped, gasped for breath. As he checked his pocket watch it clicked on to the deep red sector. He was three days behind schedule. Retirement beckoned. Tomorrow he would be 470 and this should be his last haunting. He mustn't fail. The disgrace of relegation to the headless division was unthinkable, *and* it would mean another 130 years of servitude.

The vibrations emanated from the young man at the desk. Mervin chuckled. He'd found his client. He switched off his locator. This modern idea of multi-tasking was such a drain on one's resources. Unable to manifest without total darkness, he settled on a cushion of air, amused himself by observing the antics of the humans.

'Watch it!' Susan said. 'You're spreading Uncle Bert on the floor.'

John glared at his sister. 'I haven't touched anything.'

Her eyes widened as she watched the canister leak its contents.

'Stop playing the fool,' she said with a shudder. 'It's not funny.'

John raised his hands in haunting mode. 'Oooooh.'

She dug him in the ribs. 'Pack it in.'

Mervin shook his head. It's merely tomfoolery. Why request a haunting?

'Looks like we needn't trail up to the Oak Wood,' John said with a laugh. 'Uncle Bert's settled for being scattered on the old oak floor.'

Susan grabbed the canister, tried to twist the lid.

'This lid *is* on tight,' she said. 'I can't move it.'

John held out his hand. 'Give it here. It's probably cross-threaded.'

A fash on the lid gouged his finger, drew blood, but the lid didn't budge.

'It took us three hours to get here,' he said with a yawn, as he flopped spread-eagled on the sofa. 'It felt like another three, traipsing there and back to the crematorium. Then we had to listen to pages of bequests and conditions. I vote we eat first. Sort the stuff out this afternoon, then stay here overnight.'

She raised her eyebrows. 'What turned you into a grouch?'

John's stomach rumbled.

'Okay, I get the picture.' Susan laughed as she opened the larder door. 'You'll not get fat on this lot. There's a packet of whiskery sausages, two eggs, laid last year, some rancid butter, a hunk of mouldy bread. Ugh!' She shuddered. Pulled a face, quickly turned her head away. 'And some sour milk.'

'What did the old boy live on?'

'Not much by the look of it,' she said. 'I'll nip to the shop.'

Twenty-five minutes later, Susan rushed in, breathless, yet pale.

'Last night, a girl was chased by a large animal,' she said. 'They say it escaped from the safari park.'

'The old boy would have loved that – going on safari,' John said. He stood up, took aim with an imaginary rifle. 'Pow! Pow! I bet that's why he lived out here.'

She threw a cushion at him. 'Can't you ever be serious?'

They spent the remainder of the day putting aside the bits of furniture and ornaments their uncle had bequeathed to various individuals. Piles of junk, piles for the charity shop, a few items they decided to keep. The rest, mostly furniture, would go to auction.

Mervin was becoming restless. All this materialistic nonsense was so boring. He wished they would make less noise so that he could have a snooze.

After supper, Susan stood in front of the door.

'Don't go out tonight,' she said.

John pulled a gruesome face, lifted his arms.

'Ooooooh.'

'Pack it in,' she said. 'It's a big old house, I don't want to be alone.'

'Well Uncle Bert won't come and get you, his ashes are sprinkled about, the old boy won't be able to manifest properly. Of course, he could be headless,' John said, 'but I'm betting he's armless.'

She threw a cushion at him. Was just about to follow it with another when there was a loud hammering on the door. With a push from his sister, John went to admit their visitor.

The local policeman followed him back into the room.

'You must be Miss Susan,' the bobby said. 'We heard all about you both from Bert. I saw your car as I was passing. If I'd known you were staying here after the funeral, I would have come earlier.'

'It was a last minute decision,' John said, 'to save us coming back next weekend.'

'Well, I came to warn you,' the constable said.

'I was in the village earlier,' Susan said, '*is* there an animal loose?'

'Marie said an animal chased her,' the constable said. 'Her friend saw something too. She said it was hazy, but she was certain it was a bear. We're treating it seriously. Farmers and park rangers have been searching all day, some are still out there. The trackers say there's no sign of any large animal having been in the area.'

That's strange, Mervin thought. *I'm* supposed to do the animal haunting. He concentrated, failed to make contact. I'll bet the telepathic communication lines are down again, he muttered. It's a shambles. That new chap isn't up to standard.

The policeman walked towards the door.

'I shouldn't go out this evening, if I were you,' he said, 'especially now it's almost dark.'

'Thank you for calling, and don't worry,' Susan said, with a meaningful look at her brother, 'we won't be going out.'

After the policeman left, Susan pointed to the battalion of bolts on the door.

'Push those top ones over, John,' she said. 'It's best to be sure. We must check the back door as well, and all the windows.'

After Susan went to bed, John quietly slid back the bolts on the front door. He stepped out. Locked the door behind him.

He must be one of those city types, always in need of entertainment, Mervin thought as he floated after him towards the village.

The only action John saw was a game of dominoes at the "Dog and Rabbit". He bought a bottle of whisky, returned to Uncle Bert's house and started working his way down the bottle.

Mervin yawned. He was a bit long in the mantle for all that gallivanting. He soon fell asleep but the first strike of the grandfather clock jolted him. The second woke him totally. He stretched, changed shape a few times. Now refreshed, he was ready to complete his mission.

After drifting up the stairs, there was no point using unnecessary energy, he scraped and shuffled along the landing.

'John,' Susan said, her voice heavy with sleep, 'is that you?'

Mervin shambled closer, made the sounds of dragging footsteps.

'John,' she called. 'John! Stop acting the fool.'

At first, Mervin didn't utter a sound. Then he flung open her bedroom door. Susan was wide-awake, goggle eyed. His large irregular manifestation entered her bedroom, lumbered to the foot of her bed.

She screamed.

The large animal loomed over her, saliva dripped in viscous globules. She tried to edge away, but fear had frozen her muscles. Terror petrified her bones. Mervin created reeking breath as he bent over her. Her screams choked in her gullet, almost suffocated her. He gave one last howl, which caused her to faint.

What a good haunting! Mervin congratulated himself. All that remained was to let his client know that the job was complete.

Downstairs, he found John, collapsed, snoring blissfully on the sofa. Probably the lad had been unwilling, or unable, to climb the stairs in his drunken state. This was going to be a test of his powers. He needed to awaken the boy without scaring him. He blew in his ear, again and again. Finally, the human stirred.

Mervin stood close by. Appeared as a plump little fellow. He gave John a wink, a smile and a thumb's up sign. John shook his head. Rubbed his eyes, looked again. The elderly ghost, now de-materialised, had clocked off, hoping for a few more hours rest.

Next morning, Mervin stirred with the first ring of the phone. The boy grunted, shifted position. How can these humans stand the incessant noise?

John sat up. His left foot twitched uncontrollably, then made scratching movements towards his chest. Finally, he answered the phone.

Mervin hovered by the receiver, listening to the conversation.

'I'm speaking from the Grange Psychiatric Hospital,' the phone voice said. 'This is very difficult ... I'm afraid there has been a mistake. You have ... that is ... they gave you the wrong canister. I have here the canister inscribed with the name *Bertram Ffitch*. I would have rung before, but one of our patients is ... er ... missing. Could you possibly return the canister?'

'Sure. No problem,' John said. 'Hey, hang on. Whose canister do we have?'

'The remains of one of our patients.'

'Who?' John said, a note of intrigue in his voice.

'I shouldn't really say...'

'Come on,' John said, 'what's the story? You'll have to tell me if you want the canister back.'

'Very well,' the voice said. 'The man was delusional. A cat clawed his arm. He maintained that he had been contaminated. Believed that he would become an animal himself. Nothing we said could shake his belief. Nor were we able to put an end to the taunts he received from one of the other patients. It was tragic.'

★ ★ ★

It's one thing to be caught eavesdropping, quite another to be grabbed by one's mantle. Mervin quaked. Hoped the general didn't smell his fear. He was hauled back, his feet, if he had any, hardly touching the ground.

'You imbecile,' the ghostmaster general said as a dark shade of puce permeated his ghostly shroud. 'Don't you know the difference between a live human and the cremated remains? You've been following its ashes about.'

Mervin quivered like a green jelly.

'You should have known better, at your age' the general said. 'However, it appears you are exonerated. The telepathic communications sergeant failed to advise you of the client's demise. He also managed to entangle the whole telepathic network, rendering the system useless. In an effort to cover up his error, he despatched young Oona. She grasped the wrong end of the spectral plain and briefly turned the man into a grizzly bear instead of haunting him. The confused man is still wandering about.'

'That explains why I couldn't communicate,' Mervin muttered.

'We will present a united front at the All Souls meeting,' the general said. 'No doubt, psychic whispers will blow this incident out of all proportion. The city division will laugh, call us country bumpkins.' He paused. Glared in the direction of Oona and the sergeant. 'Afterwards, heads will roll. Make no mistake. Heads will roll.'

Mervin heaved a sigh of relief. A sigh so deep, that he almost dissolved into a mist. Thank goodness I am retiring, he thought. They are employing anybody these days and this department is definitely in decline.

SONGS OF THE SEA

As a child, I was unable to understand. Later, when the words gained significance, it was too late ... nobody talked about it any more. I believed that I hated the sea, believed that *I* was the reason that Mum didn't take us there on holiday. She always took my younger brother and me to stay with her sister, in the countryside. And it was during one of Dad's rare visits to my aunt's house that I learned a terrible secret. Dad had several mistresses.

Did he only pretend to go to sea? Did he visit *them* on the occasions when we were at school and couldn't wave him goodbye from the dockside? Mum kept a tight face and an even tighter temper. And when we did see him off, what then? Was the glint in his eye there because he would visit his mistresses in foreign ports? Didn't he know, or care, that Mum wept and wailed and wouldn't be comforted for days? It was no wonder that on his brief home visits Mum often cried and ranted, telling him that he neglected her.

Dad had long reclined in the arms of his maker and, when Mum was on the way to join him, I took her hand gently and asked why Dad had treated us so badly.

Even in her weak state, her eyes opened wide. Was

she surprised that I knew, or shocked that I should mention it. But I needed to know, and she was the only one who could tell me. I stroked her hand, softened my voice and told her that, when I was younger, I had heard them arguing. Heard the talk about mistresses.

She smiled. Warmth and love flooded her eyes.

'Daniella, your Dad's mistresses were the seven seas.' As death stood at the helm, a reedy laugh shook her frail body.

I didn't find it amusing. Throughout those years I'd believed Dad had wanted to be away from us because he loved other people more than he loved us. A miss-planted seed had grown into a misunderstanding. Now that I knew the truth, I realised I didn't hate the sea at all. However, I needed to confront this sea that was all-important to my father, needed to know, to understand why he found it so irresistible.

During my first visit to the coast, the sea began calling me. At first, I ignored the whisperings. But the saltiness travelled on the breeze, blew in my ear and sucked at my mouth. Wheeling over the promenade in search of scraps, the squall of the seagulls implored me to join them. I paddled at the water's edge. Sand wriggled between my toes, the ebbing waves tugged my feet. A swell rolled in from the horizon to swamp my thoughts. As the waves crested and broke, they sang about the oceans' mysteries. They invited. Cajoled.

The call of the sea was irresistible. I joined a disparate group of holidaymakers at the quayside. We filled the small boat and, with one fisherman at the tiller, it cut through the incoming tide. Meanwhile the other man baited lines and, no doubt took stock of his would-be fisher folk.

Some poor landlubber regurgitated his lunch, while everyone else held their lines loosely, anticipated their success. An excited young boy hauled in the first fish, soon followed by someone else's shout of pride as he reeled in his catch. I caught a codling, but my mounting excitement was nothing to do with the poor fish; it was the feel of ever-moving water under the hull of the boat. The pitch and toss of the bows in the swell, the yaw of the boat as an unexpected side wave struck us amidships ... that's what captured my imagination. I fell for it all. Hooked for eternity.

My week's holiday ended. Those brief bonds with the sea tried to entangle me, keep me there, but I wrenched myself free and reluctantly returned home. The job to which I returned was more boring than I remembered it to be. I scanned the newspapers, found more agreeable employment. But again, after a short spell, I was bored. I tried to concentrate on one job after another. Nothing interested me. Nothing filled that aching void. Nothing excited the pit of my stomach as much as the thought of going on an ocean voyage. I wasn't content with a cruise round the Mediterranean Islands like most first-time voyagers. Even the popular fly-cruise held no appeal. I wanted adventure. Real adventure! But first, I needed to travel as an ocean-going passenger so I could savour every moment of day and night.

Islands and coastlines of far-flung lands were weaving their magic. Calling. Beckoning. Asking with impatience why I had not visited their shores. It wasn't a question of *if* I go, but when. I saved the fare. Andrew, my younger brother, shook his head in dismay. He didn't understand, didn't share my yearning. But then, he hadn't known the secret and didn't need to understand Dad's passion.

The day arrived. Passport clutched, I boarded. Andrew was there to wave me off, but sadness tinged the day. Try as I might, I could not obliterate the memory of standing, like Andrew, on the dockside, waving goodbye to my father. I couldn't ignore the remembered hollow feeling in my stomach ... he was leaving us again. He was away most of the time. At school, children picked on me for not having a father. However often I denied it, they wouldn't believe me. I turned instead to art. Pencils, watercolours and countless pads of drawing paper were my constant companions.

The movement of the ship returned me to the present. I looked down. Saw Andrew. With arms like ensigns in a gale, I waved. Then wondered if it would be the last time I would see my brother. I knew my lust for the sea would not stop at one voyage. Someone would reward my eagerness with a job at sea. Any job at sea! As the ship nudged out of the harbour, my brother became part of the crowd, indistinguishable. I had a brief twinge of emptiness ... I was alone. Then jellyfish squirmed in my stomach, sent signals of anticipation and excitement fluttering to my mind. My resolution was strong. Nothing would have made me turn back, just as nothing could prevent those young eels from making the same journey across the Atlantic to the Sargasso Sea. It's stronger than compulsion, stronger than instinct ... its life or death. And I was determined to live.

We steamed out of Southampton. I said goodbye to Britain ... and to land. The sea called, entangled its watery web within my soul. I tried to gather my thoughts as I turned to my sketchpad. It accompanied me everywhere, together with my watercolours and a 2B pencil. Throughout my life, I packed them before my clothes. What are clothes compared to life's artistic companions? I starting making sketches of the vessel, and, always keeping a discreet distance, many of the passengers and crew.

We left the English Channel behind, crossed the Bay of Biscay. And the sea sang her song of welcome to me. As all trace of land disappeared, the sea's voice became stronger, overpowering. How could anyone resist her songs?

Hour upon hour, I stood at the ship's rail. Stared into the depths, mesmerised by the blues and greens as they wove intricate patterns. In my mind the sea lived. She was a gigantic slumbering creature, the rhythmic rise and fall of her breathing caused the undulation of the sea's surface. Her movements were words of comfort, words of understanding, words of encouragement.

Other times, I gazed towards the horizon where sea and sky confused the eye into believing they merged as one. Watercolours replaced my pencils. I washed one colour into another as I craved to capture the breathtaking sunsets that demanded I express their beauty. A beauty offset and yet enhanced by the mysteries of the ever-changing sea. And the sea sang her approval. Whispering waves eddied down the side of the ship. The churning wake shouted that she would return in another form, another day.

A school of dolphins rode alongside. They flipped and rolled, chased and played in the swell before diving back into the depths. How I yearned to join them, become part of their family, to go on a journey underwater, to see what they saw, feel what they felt. Be part of the ocean.

Then one morning without warning, the sea changed. Her palette of blues and greens vanished. Blacks, greys and whites dominated. With menace and malignance, she whipped up foam-topped rollers, sent them thundering into the maelstrom. The sea no longer crooned her sweet song of welcome. Like a woman possessed, she now showed her darker side, the thrashing, crashing and moaning of an Atlantic storm.

I held tightly to the ship's rail. Looked down. There

was no feeling of beauty, no depths inviting the eye. The dolphins were long gone. Gone to friendlier waters where they could frolic undisturbed. Sea and sky became indistinguishable, the grey of one soaking up the grey of the other. The slumbering beast had woken, gone on the rampage. Rain lashed the decks. I hung on, wanted to be part of her every mood. But, on the captain's command, the crew intervened. I was the last passenger they chivvied below deck.

In spite of the bad weather, or perhaps because of it, I still felt as one with the sea. After all, don't *we* have our moods, our sudden spits and fits of temper? And so it is with the sea. She has her off days too; days when it would be better it we kept out of her way. Unless of course, one was a sailor.

I understood the sailors' need to conquer the sea, and I now knew that my father's feelings were as deep as the ocean and equally intractable. Going to sea was his life. He couldn't give it up. Even the thought of living on land would have haunted his dreams, taunted his every hour until desolation claimed his soul. Mother never understood. And that was her loss. It was also the foundation of the misunderstanding, the occasion when I overheard them talking and learned the secret. At least Dad talked. Mum shouted and wept and said he loved his mistresses more than he loved her.

But my child's mind had taken everything literally ... Dad didn't love Mum! I couldn't forget the other word, kept it secret until I understood its meaning. By then, I'd forgotten the context. My growing-up self only remembered the previously unknown word. As far as I was concerned, Dad had mistresses. How uncomplicated are childish minds, how little adults realise that they need plain speech? I wish I'd known the truth.

Only now did I understand Dad's fascination with the sea. His mistresses were ancient, yet every swell, each wave was newborn, fascinating, tantalising. Had I known, I would have teased him, out of Mum's earshot of course, asked which mistress he would visit on his next voyage, which ocean or sea. He would have sat me on his knee, or as I grew older, sat opposite me by the fire, and told me stories of his maritime adventures. And I would have dreamed of sailing the seas that I had come to love. But there had been no stories. No talk of the sea.

Below deck, I listened. Found the unruliness of the pounding sea to be comforting, as though it understood. Perhaps it did. Was that why it thrashed and raged in bewilderment of humanity?

Tantrum over, the storm blew itself out, the sea settled back into her otherworldly life. Became the perfect mistress. Once more, she created patterns of blues and greens; different patterns with each rise and fall of her aquatic breathing. And I was part of her, just as my father had been ... part of her and through her, all life. I had found my destiny, found my place in society, a place that the songs of the sea made beautiful and enchanting.

SHOWTIME!

Rob was a good mate. A tall guy, six three, butch as they come, but he was a bit too straight. We were all up for a good laugh. But somehow you felt that it was like having your maiden aunt tagging along. The nearer the knuckle a joke was, the less he laughed. Back in the late sixties, in Oz, you could have plenty of fun, if you were in the know.

He should have had a class job, not stuck with us on a building site. Rob knew more than the rest of us put together. I never once saw him read, not even a newspaper. It didn't figure.

One night, when we were kicking our heels, Rob said, 'Let's grab a few tinnies and crash a beach barbie.'

I pulled a face. 'Nah, that's a bit tame,' I said. 'Let's go down the red-light district. We haven't been there for months. I reckon it'd be good fun. See what crawls out of the woodwork.'

'You wouldn't say that, Jimmy, if it were your sister,' Rob said.

'It's a bit late for our Maggie to flog her mutton,' I said with a wink. 'She's six months gone.'

'Or your mother?'

'Leave off.' I grinned. I was trying *not* to picture my old Ma on the streets.

We headed off to Bondi. I trawled around for a while. Didn't make out. The tucker was great. We stuffed ourselves with seafood and anything else they shoved on the barbie. The music was just how we liked it. Ear splitting, so the whole of Sydney could enjoy it. We drank our fill of the beer, lager and cider that flowed freely. Later, with a full moon that stage-lit the swell of the ocean's big dumpers, the kids shrieked and giggled as they streaked down the beach for a spot of skinny-dipping. Afterwards, we meandered home. Set about entertaining the neighbourhood with our singing.

Rob came over all school-teacherish. 'Keep it down,' he said, 'people are sleeping.'

'Sh!' I said, holding on to one of the lads as I put my finger to my lips. 'It was a great barbie. We had a laugh. There were plenty of girls begging for it. Shame all the best talent was taken.'

Rob looked a bit narked. 'You should save yourself for the right one.'

I laughed. 'You what! Save myself! I like to spread a little happiness wherever I go, as often as I can.'

'Grow up, Jimmy! Settling down is important,' Rob said.

'For Christ's sake, Rob, we're nineteen! There's loads a time for settling down. If I looked like you, I reckon they'd be grovelling at my feet.'

He's good-looking guy and should have had the sheilas fighting over him. Now me, well I reckon a 'roo took a kick at my face. I was skinny too, a shrimpy five six with straight manky hair. I was a bit of a practical joker. Why not? You've got to make the most of what you've got.

'Have a good time, that's my motto,' I said. The lads nodded. 'Get a good chat-up line. Loosen them up with a few Snowballs or Babychams. I usually make out.'

Rob gave me a disgusted look.

He had no go in him. Know what I mean? Don't get me wrong. He's a great guy, the best. Just needed to loosen up.

While he was visiting his folks in Brisbane, we checked out the red-light district.

God, you should have clocked some of the sheilas down there. One hag looked as if she'd been at it eighty years. She smelt like a dingo's armpit and her face could have been an old loofah with make-up trowelled over the holes. But I don't suppose any of her clients noticed her face. You saw high-heels and plunging necklines. That was only the fellas! There were good lookers, scrags, young kids and weirdoes. They were all there, good and bad. Some you wouldn't touch with a surfboard. It was a right laugh.

We spotted this show. It was none of your cheap bump and grind. It was a real class act. Posh place, decked out like a music hall, that kind of set-up. The compère was a comic in ridiculous drag. He practically fell on to the stage as he tripped up on his oversize shoes. His jokes came thick and fast. He had us in stitches.

Then it went as quiet as a reef with a shark on the prowl. All eyes swivelled forward left as the strippers came on. Gorgeous they were. Long legs balanced on heels the height of ships' masts. Could they strut their stuff! I remember one, in a plain dress, sang "Second-hand Rose". Course, we knew they weren't actually singing. Back then, even most of the Aussie TV stars mimed to US or Pommy records.

The others had long posh frocks and puffed out wigs. Some wore sparkly headdresses, others had coloured emus' feathers. They looked eight feet tall! Done up to the nines they were. They all sang as they stripped. Some did a double-act. Trouble was you couldn't scrape your eyes from one to get a good gander at the other. They all ended up practically topless. Most of them could have done with a boob-job. Shame there wasn't much of that done back then! What they lacked up top they certainly made up for in the "tease" part. They knew all the moves, and some! You felt they were singing just for you. Inviting you. You wanted to reach out, to grab a handful.

After every act, the comic was back. He brought you down to earth. The next stripper got you going again. Each time his rig-out kit was more outrageous than the last. One of his get-ups was Scottish. He wore a bright orange wig, topped by a tartan bonnet. The house almost caved in when he showed what Scotsmen wear under their kilts!

At the interval, the sheilas strutted up the aisles and there we were, stuck in the middle of a row. No chance to chat any up.

The next night, we didn't make that mistake! We were first in the queue.

'I'll toss you for the end seat,' I said as I took out my old two-headed penny. 'I'll take heads.'

The routines were just as good the second time around. I nabbed one of the sheilas as she walked up the aisle. She was a looker, best of the lot. You could smell the greasepaint mixed with her scent. The stuff of her dress kind of rustled. Even that was a come-on.

I smiled. Opened my mouth, determined to give her my best chat up line. She ignored me.

When she walked back for the finale, I said, 'What about tomorrow, then?'

She tipped me the wink. We were on.

We met after the show. God was she a stunner! Long platinum blonde hair, all done up on top in elaborate swirls. Pools of sea-blue eyes swallowed me up. She wore scent that screamed, "Come and get me". Her make-up looked as if she'd been done up for the movies. Her legs were so long that they climbed right up to heaven.

Trouble was Angelina, God's gift of an angel, didn't fancy me. It was hardly surprising. In those high heels she was a good eight inches taller than me. There was more to her than that though. She had a great personality, with a fantastic sense of humour. And she was a real sport. Would have suited Rob.

'My mate should have been here,' I said. 'He doesn't know what he's missing. He's a great guy, you'd love him.'

I told her all about Rob. I think I cracked it, when she realised he wasn't an ugly runt like me. Her eyes twinkled wickedly. She gave me a funny kind of smile, coy, but willing.

I decided to push my luck. 'Let me set up a meeting with Rob when he gets back from Brisbane.'

'Oh, I don't know,' she said.

By then she was laughing. I knew I'd won her over. She agreed to meet Rob after the show the following week.

I picked a class bar for the meeting. Just outside the red-light district. Didn't want him looking down his nose. All we had to do was convince Rob that this gorgeous sheila wanted to meet him.

He looked more at ease when he got back. I reckon he must have needed that break. I wasted no time.

'I've been trying to get off with this sheila,' I said.

Rob laughed. 'Only trying? What's up, Jimmy? Lost your touch?'

'Straight up,' I said. 'Her name's Angelina. I fancied her rotten as soon as I clapped eyes on her. She's real shy. Took me ages to suss that she'd had her eye on *you* for weeks before you went away.'

I told him all about her, except the strip-joint part. The lads gathered round, made envious noises.

Rob's eyes were on stalks. 'Great. When do I meet her?'

★ ★ ★

I'd sorted out our lookout spot in advance. We crouched behind some greenery, waited for the action. Rob was early. He'd sure loosened up. That was no surprise, after the billing we gave her. Done up for a wallaby's wedding, he was. His aftershave surfed in across the room, hit us full on the nose. He put a couple of records on the jukebox, then sat in the alcove at the table we'd reserved.

As Shirley Bassey belted out "Big Spender", Angelina walked in, minus the feathers. Heads turned. She was a knockout. Kind of slow and slinky, she walked over to Rob, her hips swaying to the music.

We could hardly keep quiet. Nothing happened! They sat there, heads close together, talking. It looked as if they were getting on great. Come on, Rob, get your glasses on mate! Then I twigged it. I realised why he never read. Why he never tried for a good job. The bloody fool's short-sighted! That *must* be it.

The sheilas from that show were absolute stunners. Shapely. Great legs. The thing is, they were all fellas. Transsexuals, cross-dressers, drag queens, who knows? Maybe they *did* have implants or injections. They had this wired "U" shape, like a bra with no material, just tassels. Maybe it just pushed up their own flesh. Whatever! They could sure make those tassels swirl!

Rob stood up. Angelina joined him. They walked out together, arm in arm. Bloody hell! I got up sharpish. Nearly sliced my cheek on a pad of prickly pear. I caught them as they were leaving.

God, this is going to be awkward, I thought. 'Rob, mate...'

'You've met Richard,' Rob said. He put his big mitt on the gorgeous Angelina's shoulder. 'He told me about the set-up when I phoned him before I left Brisbane. Great gag, Jimmy, one of your best.'

I stared, confused.

Rob laughed. 'We've been seeing each other secretly for six months. That's why I cleared off to Brisbane, to see if I could forget him. I can't. We're moving in together. Sorry mate. The sting's on you. We set you up good and proper.'

I gawped like a shark that's had its tucker snatched.

CHAMELEON

I transformed myself. Became a barn owl. Glided down on silent wings, a ghostly image in the fading light. I laughed at the moon. Laughed at its feeble attempt to shed light in the misty glade. Hidden from unwanted eyes, I waited within the haze. This was our secret rendezvous, secluded, ideal for lovers. Brad *would* come. He loved me. Now, I must show him the way. Help him to believe. Only he has the power to change my fate. Enable us to spend eternity together.

He parked the car. Doused the lights. I froze. A girl was with him. Jealousy raged within me. My anger gained momentum. Vengeance followed in its footsteps. Over-ran my commonsense. Now, they would both pay.

I entered the body of a mosquito, flew closer. Found an open window. The girl felt nothing as I sank the mosquito's proboscis into her young skin.

'Come on, Allie,' Brad said to her, 'stop sulking.'

I abandoned the mosquito to its own affairs, hovered around the girl. I had another trick, one that I intended to use by slow degrees. My feelings were confused, I loved him, believed he loved me, but I felt betrayed too. Felt the need to punish him. I changed her dark, velvet-brown eyes to hazel. He blinked. Edged closer. Squinted at her face. I glowed with satisfaction. He was transfixed.

She scowled. 'What are you staring at?'

He bit his lip. Furrowed his brow. 'Can't I look at you?'

I faded those irian glints of yellows and greens. Allie fluttered her lashes. Fish cold eyes stared out. Blues and greens now dominated.

The moon, wanting no part in my plan, snared a passing cloud. Skulked above it. Sulked with downcast mouth.

Brad shut his eyes. He triangled the bridge of his nose between his index fingers.

Allie nudged his arm. 'Now what's up?'

'Nothing.' He shrugged. Faked a yawn. 'It's been a rough week.'

Nearby, a barn owl screeched. Like a wailing banshee, its mate replied.

To spook Allie further, I sent a shiver down her spine.

She shuddered. Rubbed her hands up and down her arms. 'Let's go. I don't like it here. It's ... creepy. Besides, it's only eight-thirty. There's still time to go to that dance.'

'Do we have to?'

'You promised.' She pouted, snuggled up to him. 'We could go dancing. Have a meal. There'd still be time to go back to your place.'

The thought of them together was unbearable. I entwined myself round him. Let him feel my presence, smell my body. He had a faraway look in his eyes. Yes, that's it, Brad, you're beginning to remember how it was between us, aren't you?

Her face tilted. She kissed him on the cheek. His arm restrained her shoulder, prevented her lips from finding his. He *does* know I'm here ... watching. He can sense my presence. I'm sure he can.

She twisted round to face him. 'Come on, Brad, what's up?'

'Nothing ... I dunno.'

'Look at me,' she said.

He raised his head. Looked at her face. I continued to alter the colour of her eyes. Now to an inquisitive blue that pierced, prodded, questioned. Forced him to remember. I could feel his panic. I changed the girl's brown hair to black. Faded the bronzed skin to a deathly pallor. Took over her body completely.

'Now you know who I am,' I said. 'Don't you?'

Was my familiar voice so strange? I laughed at him. His eyes widened. The silence was eerie, broken only by the quickening thunder of his heartbeat.

'How the hell?' He swivelled round. Saw the empty back seats. 'Where's Allie?'

'Gone,' I said. 'She tried to take *my* place with you. I couldn't allow that.'

'But...' Brad paled. His eyes widened into the hypnotic stare of a cornered rabbit. Confusion strangled his words. 'Sylvie ... you ... you died.'

'What *is* death? Merely a word without meaning,' I said. 'Besides, I was only away for a while.'

'Six months.' His voice was flat, automated.

That hurt. Didn't he care? But I could tell he wasn't his normal self. He was still in shock, I suppose.

'Who's counting? Exactly a year ago,' I said, 'you waited until the stroke of midnight and then proposed to me. Today, they allowed me to return. It's the vernal equinox. You mortals don't know that it's a magical time, do you? Of course, now I'm here, I might stay indefinitely. Unless you want to come back with me.'

'Okay, a joke's a joke, but that's enough. It's not funny.' I'd always thought of him as more of an active guy, not too good with words. Maybe I was wrong. 'Take the wig off, and the coloured contact lenses. You'd never be a match for Sylvie.'

He reached for my hair. Pulled.

I smiled. This was more like it; I was getting through to his emotions. 'We came here, right to this spot. You swore we would be together. Forever.'

I sent a worm of guilt to nip his gut.

'This isn't happening,' he said, 'It was just a bad seafood salad at lunchtime.'

I grinned. 'Was it?'

He risked a glance at my face.

'It *is* me,' I said, 'I'm back.'

'I *did* love Sylvie,' he said.

He sounded enthusiastic. Or was it merely an act. I

needed convincing. Did he really love me? I leaned forward. Kissed him, long and hard. He responded, perhaps out of habit. I was inviting, warm and soft, wafting his favourite perfume: *Spring Jewels,* towards his nose.

He broke away. Turned to face me. 'Get off! This is crazy. It's a nightmare.' He grappled with the door handle.

I jammed the door shut.

'Let me out!' Frantically, he thumped the car horn ... of course I prevented it from emitting any sound. 'Oh, God, this isn't happening.'

I touched his arm.

He turned to me. 'Okay. What do you want?'

Was he coming round, recognising the truth? I smiled. 'You.'

'Me? So why wait all this time?'

'I desperately wanted to come before,' I said. 'I couldn't. I was serving my apprenticeship.'

Brad looked confused. Perhaps he was still trying to understand how Allie turned into me.

'I know you're trying to concentrate on Allie,' I said. 'You think that if you could get her back, everything would return to normal. Don't you?'

After several minutes, a smile curled round his lips.

'You *are* Allie, aren't you? You spiked my drink. Was I supposed to act the fool at that dance you wanted to go to? Well, I'm not buying it. You *did* spike my drink, didn't you? You little tart. This is definitely a bad trip.'

At that moment, I hated him. He was ruining everything. 'A bad trip is it? You'll see what a bad trip is. What would you like?'

He looked at me as though I was crazy.

I'll show him crazy. I laughed. Sent manic echoes reverberating round the confines of the car. Why couldn't he accept the facts? Why couldn't he believe? I've failed. If *she* hadn't been there. If I hadn't lost my temper... But she *had* been there. Now I had to show him for what I was destined. I leaned forward. Kissed his cheek. Worked my way to his mouth. He couldn't resist me. Pain constricted his throat. He fought for breath. Fumbled with the window winder. It was a puny effort against my powers. As his breathing returned to normal, panic grabbed him by the throat. He put the key in the ignition. Turned it. I ensured he only heard the groan of a dead battery.

'*I* made your throat sore,' I said. That got his attention.

'Oh yeah?' He looked at me as if I was dirt. 'My throat only seemed sore because the air in the car is dry. You're not real.'

In a fit of delicious spite, I punished him by putting my hand on his face. Sent hot shivers through his body. Beads of sweat united into salty runnels. His temperature soared. He almost lost consciousness.

I laughed. 'Have you had enough?'

He tried to speak. When his voice refused to cooperate, he pleaded with his eyes.

I shook my head, raised an eyebrow. 'You haven't got much resistance, have you?'

His temperature dropped. He looked in the mirror. Felt his face.

'Normally, we can't infect anyone we know, but I was a brilliant student,' I said. 'I learned all the secrets.' All the secrets, I thought, except how to stop loving somebody.

'Come off it. You expect me to believe that? It's the drugs talking. I'm only sweating because you're freaking me out.'

'I can give you any infectious or communicable disease known to man. *And* some that are still unidentified. What would you like? Shall I give you scarlet fever, mumps or maybe typhus? Or what about a good dose of the plague?'

His eyes widened. Had he finally realised that everything was real? That I was real? He grabbed the door handle. Rattled it frantically. With shaking fingers, he turned the ignition key again. The engine growled in protest. He reached down. Spread his fingers. Searched.

'If you're looking for that safety device for cutting seat belts and smashing the window in an emergency, you'll not find it,' I said. 'There is no way out. Unless *I* let you out.'

Brad looked me straight in the eye. 'You wouldn't hurt me,' he said. 'We had something special.'

He was right. We did. The problem was I still loved him. Wanted him. But my life was in the balance. He *must* believe in me, in our future together. Then I would escape from a terrible fate.

'Okay,' he said. 'Let me get this straight. You came back, a carrier for all these diseases, and changed Allie's body to look like you?'

'Right,' I said. Finally, he was taking it seriously. 'I can change my body into whatever I choose ... or enter any living form.'

'Why?' He looked hurt, as though it was my fault, my decision. 'I mean, why go about spreading diseases? And why you?'

I took a deep breath. It was against the rules, but I had nothing to lose. 'Very few are chosen. Have you ever heard of Typhoid Mary?'

'Who the hell's Typhoid Mary?'

'At the beginning of the last century, a girl called Mary Mallon started a typhoid epidemic in New York. Didn't you see the film about her?'

Brad shrugged.

'It wasn't a bad interpretation. At least they got it right that she worked in a bakery. Stupid cow. Then again, she probably didn't even know that she was a carrier. Some novices don't. But she could only pass on typhoid. Unlike her, I control and carry *all* diseases. How else do you think we keep humanity in check? What if, each person, instead of dying of a sickness, had lived? Imagine the millions of extra descendants. People would overrun the earth. Cause famine and drought. Now do you see?'

He was calming down. Giving the impression that he wanted to understand.

An owl hooted plaintively. The moon, paler now, sent a shower of disapproving silver light. It balanced in the treetops. Gazed at me reproachfully. Had my explanation overstepped the mark? Would they punish me?

I was fighting back tears. 'You couldn't stay faithful. Could you? Not even for six months.'

Brad turned to me, his eyes full of love and longing. 'I'll always love you, Sylvie,' he said. 'When you died, I was desperately lonely. I only buried myself in the arms of other girls to try to forget you.'

He leaned over me. Brushed away my tears. Kissed me gently. I smiled at him. Accepted that his love was strong. The car accident wasn't his fault. I had been driving. I was the one over the limit. After the crash, he'd tried to save me. It was too late. Why didn't he have that same enthusiasm now? Why can't he believe that we could be together? But he didn't believe, not enough. Not enough to ensure our future together. Not enough to snatch me from eternal damnation.

I wanted him to be happy. I realised that the greatest test of love was to know when to let go. Allie slept, she would remember nothing. I sighed. She wasn't the girl for him, but someone else would be. I kissed Brad gently. He was free. Free to find another love. What more could I ask for?

Jutting from beneath a cloud, the moon's yellow

grin approved. From a nearby tree, the barn owl called to its mate. She joined him. They flew off together, paired for life. I accepted my fate and would follow the course for which I was destined. Taking a different form, I would choose, at random, those I would infect.

WORD PERFECT

François, the eminent plastic surgeon, doted on his clientele, danced attendance to their every need. His clinic was akin to a five-star hotel, where patients were cosseted during their recovery period.

Only one fly tainted his operations ... Marianne. She was never satisfied. He felt obliged to cater to her whims since she was married to one of the most respected members of his club. She was not, of course, aware of this connection.

'You are the greatest plastic surgeon,' Gidor, the husband, said, when he first approached François. 'I would consider it a personal privilege if you would allow my wife to consult with you.'

Without hesitation, François agreed. Many times since, he wished he had made some excuse, but how could he?

'My face is perfect,' Marianne said at their first meeting. 'I will have a breast implant.'

She threw him off guard. In all his experience, no patient had ever used that tone with him. 'Your figure is perfectly formed,' he said. 'You do not need any enhancements.'

'How dare you! How dare you tell me what I need?

I will come into the clinic next Thursday. You may operate the next day.'

François checked his diary. Remembered Gidor. Sighed in resignation. Pencilled her in. 'That's arranged. You will be here for three days.'

She glared at him. 'I will be here until the swelling has subsided and the scars have healed. I will not step outside until then. Well! What are you waiting for? Ensure that my room will be available. My husband will pay.'

They discussed, at least Marianne demanded, the size of her implant, and then with a twirl and a waft of heady perfume, she waltzed out. François flopped back in his chair. How could Gidor, so aristocratic, so considerate, have managed to become ensnared by that woman? He thought out his options, soon realised that there weren't any.

On the appointed day, Marianne strode into his office. 'See that my bags are taken to my room.'

He considered telling her that his nurses were not porters, but thought better of it. After all it was a one-off and he would give his staff an extra bonus for the period she remained in their care.

Later, he visited her room.

'Remove that wall mirror! And take away the hand mirror, too. I do not wish to see any part of my body until it is in perfect order.'

'Certainly, I understand,' he said. 'This is the consent form, which I would be obliged if you would sign.'

She raised her eyebrows. 'I...'

'It is standard procedure,' he said, '*and* the law. I must have your consent in writing before I begin the operation.'

After reading the document, twice, she took out her gold pen and signed her name.

'Perhaps you would like to come down for dinner?'

That was his big mistake. He soon realised that he should have pandered to her vanity and allowed his staff to wait on her in her own room.

A young girl awaiting surgery on her disfigured face was approaching the dining room.

Marianne stared. 'Surely you aren't going to dine with the other patients? Your face is enough to curdle the milk.'

The girl burst into tears. From his office, François had heard the exchange and rushed out. He took the girl to one side.

But Marianne hadn't finished. 'After he has made your face respectable, you should have him do your hips. They're too fat.'

François swallowed his bile. Turned his back on the woman who aspired to greatness but had the social charms of a toad. Then with a brief apology to all toads, he put his arm round the girl and escorted her to her room.

'Take no notice,' he said. 'She is an ignorant arrogant woman and, sooner or later, she will trip up on her evil tongue.'

Through her sobs the girl managed a smile. It wasn't his normal practice to criticise one patient in front of another, but this was an exception. The girl was one of François' special patients. That's how he preferred to categorise those who were in need of surgery, those that the National Health sector referred as "deserving" cases.

And that is how the situation continued with Marianne. There was always something that needed his immediate attention, and there was always somebody she cut into during her stay. His staff dreaded her arrival, celebrated her departure. What's more other ladies who were his patients from time to time started to ask if the coast was clear. He understood. It was a traumatic time, a time of nerves, hopes and fears ... not a time to have some acerbic bitch making caustic comments.

As much as was possible, he kept Marianne in her room under the premise that she was a special patient and would receive the attention that a lady of her standing deserved. And he meant every word of it. Except that he was not in a position to wield the deserving blow.

'I am a cultured lady,' she said on one occasion, 'I cannot be expected to mingle with the commoners. You must treat a lady of letters, like myself, with due respect.

★ ★ ★

Like a cold sore on a cur, she was back again. But this time she looked different, glowing, more full of her own importance, if that were possible.

'Madam is looking very well,' François said.

The pleasant aspect changed. 'Looking very well?' If you knew what I have been through. That dreadful, mean, nasty husband of mine has driven me to despair.' Then she smirked. 'But I will have the last laugh. I have decided to divorce him.'

François stared. Then smiled inwardly. Since she was no longer with his respected club associate, he could get rid of her. He then realised that she was still prattling on.

'... As I was saying, with money and a good solicitor, anything is possible. I will screw the bastard for every penny I can get. He is so tight-fisted, a mean, mingy, moron of a man. You should have met him. I...'

François was seething with rage. Desperately wanted to bring her down ... for his, and his colleague's sake.

'I have found two wrinkles,' Marianne said. 'An immediate operation is vital.'

Francois studied her face, found no flaw. And even if had found a flaw, he would not have admitted it. He wanted rid of her. 'Madame's face is beautiful, only a strong magnifying glass would show a wrinkle.'

She glared. 'Remove the wrinkles! Re-shape my jaw. Lift my eyelids. I demand the beauty and perfection of a Greek god. I insist that you obey me to the letter. Do you understand?'

Sudden understanding imploded within François. He nodded. 'I will add your exact instructions to the consent form. As soon as Madame signs, I will proceed.'

'I must stay here until every trace of bruising has gone...'

'But...'

'*I* now pay your exorbitant fees! And I *will* stay here.'

She was so rude, not only to him, but to his other clients, too. They were all ladies of impeccable taste, and manners, cultured ladies unused to encountering aggressive behaviour. He always shrugged his apologies and offered them a discount, or some gift by way of compensation. Many times he had tried to steer Marianne towards other surgeons, but she demanded the best. Now, finally, she had succumbed to her own inadequacies.

When his assistant had typed the consent form including Marianne's exact wording, he offered it for her signature. She complied without a murmur ... after she had read through the form, twice.

François was jubilant. He was also totally committed to meeting Marianne's demands exactly. Never before had he looked forward to having her within his establishment. He warned the nurses of her presence.

After the operation, François checked on Marianne.

'It is a success,' he said. 'I followed your instructions to the letter.'

'Such impudence,' she said. 'Only *I* can say if the operation is successful.'

For the next few weeks, she plagued the nurses with her constant demands. But this time, they were quite willing to cooperate since he had assured them that this would be the last time. And he'd promised the usual anti- Marianne bonuses.

Finally, when her face was devoid of swelling and bruising, he nodded. 'All is well, Madame.'

He handed the mirror to her. She lifted it. Stared. Screamed.

François smiled. It was a great shame. Had she requested the face of a Greek *goddess*, he would have been delighted, honoured, to recreate the face of Aphrodite. But a god's face she had demanded and a god's face she received. Besides, he thought, father Zeus had such character.

LEGACY

Jake paused in the doorway. Glanced at the gleaming plaque.

'Solicitors! Them and cops,' he muttered, 'they're all the same. Out to get you.'

The glass doors parted. He nipped inside before the automatic door changed its mind. The girl behind the desk stared, nose in the air. She stood up. Ran her hands down the creases on the tight black skirt that barely carpeted her thighs. Her lips parted, then closed. Snooty tart, Jake thought, nice legs though. He scanned the inner doors. Found the desired name: W. Fotheringham. Without a sideways glance, he ambled forward.

'Wait!' The girl wavered. Made a half-hearted move. Halted, as though afraid to leave the wooden barrier of her desk. 'You can't just walk in.'

Jake dodged past her. Pushed open the door. The solicitor jumped nervously, spilt his coffee in its saucer. Peered over his half-moon spectacles at the intruder.

The girl teetered into the room. Wrinkled her nose at Jake. Avoided contact with the interloper as she clitter-clattered towards her boss. 'He pushed past me,' she said.

'Jake Wilson,' the lad said. His matted dreadlocks hung proudly. Compensated for his attempt to grow a beard and the resulting short tufts of dirty blond hair. 'You sent for me. And I didn't do no pushing.'

'Thank you, Sue,' the solicitor said, 'that will be all.'

Jake sneaked a step behind her. 'Boo!'

She skidded on the floor. Almost fell. Regained her balance, then wobbled off hurriedly.

Jake laughed. 'Stuck up cow! She ain't got no right.' He looked the solicitor straight in the eye. 'That letter told me to come, "to my advantage", it said.'

Mr Fotheringham ran a finger under his stiff collar. Eased the folds of skin. The exertion of rising from his chair brought a flush to his face. His rotund body, encased in a black suit and waistcoat, balanced precariously on short stubby legs. He sprayed air freshener round the room. Resumed his seat.

'That's right,' Jake said, 'you get rid of that smell of coffee. It don't half pong in here.'

The lad sat. His feet beat a silent rhythm on the floor. His legs danced in unison allowing grimy knees to elbow through his jeans. He tugged at the hem of his T-shirt. The thin material fingered its way over each of his ribs. Stained cotton replaced the grey of his midriff. He leaned back. Ceased tapping. Lifted one leg, then the other, on to the desk, where his scuffed trainers sat incongruously with the highly polished desk accoutrements.

Mr Fotheringham glowered. Looked first at the

offending feet, then at Jake. He cleared his throat. With a shrug, Jake removed his feet from the desk.

'I am instructed by your late aunt,' Mr Fotheringham said, 'to inform you of your legacy.'

Jake twisted his tongue into one of his broken teeth, winkled out a piece of stale food. 'So the old gal left me something, did she?' He scraped his chair across the parquet flooring. Leaned closer. Closer, he felt, to his inheritance.

The solicitor squirmed. That is, he squirmed as much as the chair would permit, since they fitted together like walnut and shell. He read out the pertinent section of the will.

Jake's attention strayed. He waggled his forefinger in his right ear. Satisfied, he removed the finger. Inspected it. Then wiped the dross across his T-shirt. Unfamiliar words flowed over his head. He looked up.

'Come again? All that mumbo jumbo don't mean much,' he said. 'Say it proper, like what normal people talk.'

Mr Fotheringham cleared his throat. 'Quite so,' he said. 'Your aunt has been very generous. You inherit a house, complete with six lodgers and an apartment for yourself. There is a condition.' He paused. Peered over his spectacles. 'You must take care of her beloved Great Dane, Bertie.'

'What! You mean I get no dosh if I don't look after that bloody dog?'

'Exactly.'

'I hate dogs,' Jake said. 'That thing is the size of an elephant.'

'Er ... mm, let me see.' Mr Fotheringham scanned through the sheaf of papers on his desk. 'Yes,' he said, 'your aunt was most specific regarding Bertie. She has left rather complicated instructions about the manner in which he must be cared for and, in particular, his food requirements.'

Jake shrugged. 'Okay. I look after the mutt.'

'There is, of course, the matter of maintenance,' Mr Fotheringham said. 'You will be responsible. In the event that you are unable to carry out the work yourself, you may employ a tradesperson.'

'I ain't bloody useless,' the lad said.

'One other thing ... It is a little ... er ... delicate.' He peered at Jake. 'You must keep out of trouble.'

'I was fitted up for that assault charge,' Jake said. He half stood ready to defend his corner. '*I* didn't do it. False imprisonment, that's what it was. As for the other charges, well, the cops had it in for me. *And* they never pinned that knifing on me. *Because it weren't me!*'

The solicitor's face reddened. He cleared his throat. Eased his collar. 'Your aunt did stress that there must be no reverting to type,' he said. 'She had your best interests at heart, I can assure you.'

Jake gave the solicitor a look of disgust. He pocketed the set of keys. Pushed the sheaf of instructions into his pocket. Swaggered out of the office. He gave the girl a smug grin. Smirked at the automatic door. Then stepped out into the bright June sunshine.

He strutted along the pavement. Chin up, shoulders swinging. He ignored the disdainful glances from passers-by. Delighted in watching pedestrians make detours to avoid him. They don't own the place, he thought, they ain't no better than me.

The canine brute had temporarily slipped his mind. Now, it bounded back into his thoughts. He stopped suddenly. The woman behind collided with him. Dropped her shopping. Oranges rolled down the pavement. A carton gaped. Two eggs cracked open on the paving slabs, ready for frying. She stepped forward. Anger scowled her face, her mouth opened ready to place the blame. Jake gave challenging eye contact. She backed off. He walked on without a word.

'How,' he muttered, 'will it greet a relative stranger in its own territory? Will it be friendly?'

He called at a butcher's shop. Purchased some scraps of meat in the hope of bribing his giant companion. With both pockets now bulging, he continued to inconvenience the passers-by. They're lucky I haven't got my mates with me, he thought. My mates would make them scarper. Either that, or they'd rob a few pockets. The address of his new home was some distance away. Jake was in a high spirits. He thought the journey was a good opportunity to reconnoitre the area. To size up which properties were worthy of a night time raid. Perhaps passing on such information would elevate him in the gang's hierarchy.

He pushed open the front door to his new home. Inserted the key into the lock of the ground floor flat. Thunder roared from within. The floor shook. A welcoming committee was gathering momentum.

Even grounded on all four feet, the dog's uptilted face was at Jake's chest. He thought Bertie was way too friendly for a first encounter. Tried to push the dog away.

'You don't half stink,' he said, holding his nose.

A slobbering mouth snuffled at his pocket. Jake took out the butcher's parcel of bits before Bertie ate through his pocket. The dog drooled. Looked up expectantly. But he waited.

Jake opened the parcel, put it on the floor. 'Okay, boy.'

In the time it took Jake to shut the door, Bertie devoured his lunch, including part of the bloodied wrapping paper.

Followed closely by Bertie, he checked out his new home. Noticed the single mattress on the floor alongside the single bed. 'Look's like you live in comfort, Bertie,' he said.

The larder was well stocked. His eyes gleamed. Good old aunt Madge! Tins and packets rubbed cheek and jowl with doggie chocolates and a sack of dog biscuits. But there was no dog food. He fished the instructions out of his pocket. Smoothed them over.

'Steak! She fed you steak?'

In disgust, he ignored the list. Shoved the five pages of instructions back into his pocket. He turned. Bertie, two huge paws rested on the shelf, was about to help himself from the sack.

'Oi!'

Doleful brown eyes looked at him accusingly, as if to say, "You forgot to give me my biscuits".

On their first excursion to the park, Bertie could have won a rosette in the obedience class at Cruft's. He walked to heel. Sat at the pavement edge, awaited instruction. When Jake flung a stick, Bertie galloped after it, legs splayed at all angles. The lad grimaced. Clenched his teeth. Closed one eye. But the dog neatly swerved round all obstacles. The huge beast didn't flatten a single person during their playful stick-fetching exercises. Even toddling bipeds were safe from Bertie's lolloping gait and huge feet.

Eventually, the dog's tongue hung out of the side of his mouth, a large pink sponge dribbling away the excess moisture. Each time Bertie moved, more globs of saliva swung like a pearl necklace. The chain grew. A bead broke free. Splattered itself onto the nearest object. After that jaunt, Bertie revelled in a twice-daily workout in the park. It became part of Jake's new routine. As the weeks passed, dog owners gave a friendly wave. Mothers smiled.

During the first few weeks there was an adjustment from steak to off-cuts. The dog seemed none the worse for it.

'That steak must have been bad for you, Bertie. You don't stink no more.'

He looked at Bertie. The dog relaxed on its four-fifths of the sofa. Head pressed against Jake, nose nuzzled under Jake's hand.

'You're like a bloody skip,' Jake said. 'You'll swallow anything.' He obliged the dog's attention seeking and scratched behind its ears. 'Won't you, you daft old thing?'

Bertie nuzzled closer. Made contented noises as he slobbered over Jake's jeans.

'You ain't a bloody cat! Dogs can't purr. Gurring that's what it is, gurring.' He laughed at his own cleverness. Guffawed enough to shake the sofa. Bertie barked. Joined in the excitement. Started licking Jake's face.

'Hey! Watch it! I've already had one wash this month.'

Alongside the dog's lead, were several brushes, shampoo and various bottles and jars. Tentatively, he brushed the huge dog. Bertie arched his back and "gurred" with pleasure. He rubbed against Jake's knees when the brushing stopped, big brown eyes, on a level with Jake's own, appealed for more. Jake laughed. The more the dog "gurred", the more Jake brushed. Bertie's coat shone like never before.

Bertie was definitely a people-dog. Friendly with all the tenants. As he showed no interest in the front door, Jake allowed him the run of the house, including the cellar, a place Jake hadn't bothered to explore.

On the last Tuesday of September, as they left the

park, Jake spotted his old mates. They looked innocuous enough, but he knew they were waiting for the chance to grab a handbag.

He gave the lead a quick tug. 'Come on, boy!'

Bertie obeyed immediately, heeled Jake as he ducked down a convenient side street.

The next morning, after a particularly friendly tongue-washing session, Jake fingered his sparsely haired jaw line. 'You ain't doing my beard no good,' he said to Bertie.

He bought a shaver. After posing this way and that in the mirror, he decided he liked the new look. He visited a barber for the first time since his stepfather had kicked him out of the family home.

Fourteen he had been, small for his age. All that day, he had tramped the streets. At nightfall a gang accosted him. They taunted. Threatened violence if he didn't do their bidding. The most brutish of the gang grabbed him by the scruff of his neck. Jake was tired. Scared. And above all, he was hungry. They promised food. With nowhere else to go, he fell in with them, slept on the floor of the leader's run down flat.

Many were the small windows he had been pushed through in those early days, windows the owners thought were too small for villainous intruders. Later, he survived on the gang's fringe. He never succeeded in climbing above the bottom rung of their criminal ladder.

Fourteen years had passed since the night he joined

the gang. The day that had imprinted on his memory like an epitaph on a gravestone. Unbidden, a tear appeared, his throat constricted. He swallowed, sniffed back the sentiment.

'Who needs them? I'm doing okay,' he muttered, his face buried in Bertie's welcoming fur coat.

After a balmy September, October skidded in from the arctic.

'Can't have our tenants being cold,' he said to the ever-attentive Bertie.

He ventured into the cellar's murky depths. Bertie tailed him down the steps. Kept by his side. A single naked light bulb shed barely enough light to see the boiler. The grid of the coal-chute cast the only other illumination. At regular intervals, the wall beneath the chute sprouted iron bolts. Driven in, Jake supposed, to reach the grid from inside.

The boiler proved easier to light than he thought. However, Bertie didn't seem to approve of his presence in what was clearly the dog's domain. He even gave a warning growl when Jake neared one of the corners.

'What's up, boy?'

Bertie showed his teeth. Jake backed off.

The next day, Jake, torch in hand, walked towards the cellar. Bertie almost knocked him over as he bounded ahead. Jake closed the cellar door. Started down the steps. The dog was already guarding his corner. Jake took three strides. Kept his distance from

Bertie's corner. He shone the torch into the darkness. Something settled on the back of his neck. Pirouetted down his spine. Fear!

He shuddered. 'It's all right, boy,' he said.

Bertie faced him. Front legs splayed. Shoulders high, head down. Jake slid one foot forward. Bertie's growl was low in his throat. Then, showing the whites of his eyes, he glared at Jake.

'It's all right, boy,' Jake said, confused as to why his companion had suddenly decided to turn against him. 'What's up?'

The torchlight shimmered in his shaking hand. He took a couple more steps forward. Was careful not to let the beam catch the dog's eyes. Why was Bertie guarding the corner?

The outer edge of the torch beam settled on a slouched figure. Jake shone the beam across. Vacant eyes stared into space. Bertie growled menacingly. Jake froze. The dog moved in front of the body. Jake inched one foot backwards. Then another. He dare not turn his back on the dog. He almost made it to the stairs. Bertie sprang. With two bounds the dog was at the bottom step. Jake was separated from his escape route.

He sidestepped. Leapt for the iron bolts. Clambered up. Hunkered down on the topmost bolt, out of reach. Bertie lunged. Bounded up the heap of fuel. The coke heap destabilised. Erupted in an avalanche. The dog growled and yelped as it tobogganed down on its paws.

Jake lifted the iron grid. Clambered out. Tore round

to the front door. Peered through the letterbox. He sighed with relief. The cellar door remained closed. He let himself into his flat. Slammed the door. Bolted it. He leaned against it. His heart pounded. His body shook. Trying to understand what had happened, his mind somersaulted. Became entangled with mixed emotions. Finally, with a sickening lurch, realisation dawned.

'Bloody hell! Bertie could have eaten me alive, while I slept.'

Then he remembered his aunt's sheaf of instructions. They would have to wait. He knew he must call the police. The odd fight and a bit of thieving was one thing, but even *they* must know he wasn't capable of murder.

He thought about his friend, Bertie. 'You're my mate, and I ain't no grass,' he said as though talking to the absent dog, 'but this is murder. I ain't taking the rap for no murder.'

Like an old sock, something lodged in his throat. A tear escaped, ploughed down his cheek, left a pale runnel.

Sorry, old boy,' he muttered, 'there's nothing I can do.'

He dialled, gave the information requested of him. Then sat back to read his aunt's notes.

'Poor old gal,' he said. 'She must have known her number was up.'

Madge had gone to great lengths in setting out the

dog's requirements: '...*In addition to his daily steak, you must feed Bertie small pieces of liver, heart and kidney throughout each day, every week. If not...*'

Jake's hands shook. He fumbled. Licked his finger. Turned the page '...*he will become troublesome and start chewing the furniture.*'

'Furniture! But I thought...'

The tramlines between Jake's brows deepened. His thoughts stayed with his pal as he waited.

'Anyway, Bertie doesn't chew the furniture,' he said. With the dog as a constant companion, Jake had become accustomed to voicing his opinions. 'I give him a good workout twice a day. He ain't got the energy to start chewing furniture. Maybe the old gal couldn't take him out much. Maybe he was bored. Maybe...'

Inside him a worm of doubt wriggled. The evidence was downstairs, in the cellar. He'd heard about animals defending their kill. Seen it on the telly. All the same, this was Bertie. His mate.

The police arrived before he came to any conclusion.

'So, Jake,' the sergeant said. 'What have you been up to lately?'

Without waiting for a reply he beckoned one of his men. Whispered instructions. Jake watched the others, together with two dog-handlers, head towards the cellar. A forensics team made up the procession. The apartment door closed. Guarded by the burly constable.

It was unfortunate that the sergeant now investigating the cellar was the same man who had arrested Jake on more than one occasion. Jake had hoped that his bad reputation with the police might have disappeared along with his dreadlocks and facial hair. He felt deflated, certain he would not get a fair hearing.

A short while later, the police sergeant returned. Others followed behind. Jake could see one of the dog-handlers straining with Bertie on a short lead. The dog pulled hard. Dug its claws into the carpet. Tried to break free. Jake cowered against the corner of the sofa. His old mates had told him about police brutality. He'd never experienced it himself. Didn't know if it was true. But this! They couldn't set a man-eater on him. Could they?

'I ain't done nothing,' Jake said, terrified they would let Bertie loose. Terrified the dog would maul him to death. 'I ain't seen my old mates since summer. Not since I got this place. Honest! It weren't me.'

The sergeant stared at Jake. A slow smile danced tauntingly on his lips. Jake's stomach clenched. He's enjoying this, he thought. He's always had it in for me. Now he's got me nailed.

Finally the sergeant spoke. 'By the looks of the body and the clothing it appears that the victim was a down-and-out taking shelter. The dog was probably just guarding someone who had befriended him.'

Jake released a pent-up breath. He was, however,

still undecided whether, or not, the police were still toying with him. 'You mean ... Bertie didn't kill whoever's down there?'

'He won't hurt you,' the dog-handler said with a laugh. 'He's a real softy.'

Bertie was still straining on the lead. Edging closer to Jake.

A smile of relief and pure joy spread across Jake's face. He patted the sofa. 'Come on, boy!'

All Bertie needed was those words of encouragement. He tore free. Sprang onto the sofa, slobbered all over his friend.

After the police left, Jake turned back to his aunt's notes

'...I'm sure that when you get to know Bertie, you'll love him as much as I do. Then you will understand my strict instructions and forgive him for his little bad habit. Remember, none of us are perfect. I hope you will enjoy your inheritance and will benefit from your new life. Aunt Madge.'

WAY OF THE WOLF

A slow-motion bomb of words fell from the consultant's lips; it shattered our hopes, destroyed our dreams. And yet Jon-Jo's eyes remained emotionless, his face gave no hint of his inner feelings, but I was speechless, unable to accept their words. When the reality finally hit me, I wanted to lash out, to pound them with my fists, to tell them they had made a mistake. He had to live! There *had* to be a way. I would find a way. He reached for my hand, squeezed gently.

They left us to come to terms with our tragedy. I looked down at my husband and scalding tears seared my cheeks, it was impossible to dam them back. Pain contorted his face as he inched over on his hospital bed to make room for me.

'Albany, my love,' he whispered as I snuggled up, 'you have your memories ... I'll always be with you.'

I rested my head against his on the pillow. Sobs shook my body, every muscle, every bone, every bit of flesh screamed in pain. It was wrong! They should take me instead. Jon-Jo was an artist with overwhelming talent and he was the kindest, gentlest man I had ever known. I stroked his slender fingers and fought to control the tears that clearly distressed him.

Later, when the doctors returned, Jon-Jo told them that he wished to go home. It was his choice and they agreed. I felt it was the least they could do, although I was too choked to comment, too angry to look them in the face. The ambulance people made him comfortable in our bed, set up the drip stand and checked that the saline solution was delivering correctly through the cannula in his arm. It contained the morphine that was his respite from pain, although the lines that had become etched on his face during the last months showed that its effect was not great. When they left, I cuddled beside him. I would do anything to save him. Anything! But the hospital had already tried everything. There was nothing left but hope ... or a miracle.

I prepared Jon-Jo's pureed lunch, tried to make it look appetising. When he had forced down a meagre amount, I fluffed his pillows and tucked the duvet round his thin shoulders to ensure that he was warm and comfortable for his afternoon sleep. I walked aimlessly through the house, found myself in his studio. It was heartbreaking to gaze at his paintings, knowing there would be no more. One particular work drew my attention. It was the portrait he had painted of me ten years ago, when we were first married. I smiled as I remembered that day, it was the day he told me his secret. Each Jonathon Joseph Canisham painting bore a minute white wolf. Although sometimes hidden, it was always there. He said that he felt at one with the wolf, that it was the most graceful and beautiful of all animals. A sob escaped as I realised there would be no more miniature white wolves.

Then I did something I had never done before ... never dared to do. I walked over to his easel, lifted the cloth. I gasped. The glint of the eye, the look of resignation and sorrow, he had captured it to perfection. The white wolf almost walked off the canvass. Since his eyes were yellow and his chest hair brown, he was not an albino. I held the wolf's gaze and felt a solitary tear trickle down my face. Uncannily, the brown chest markings seemed to be in the same pattern as Jon-Jo's own chest hair. It was as Jon-Jo had said, part of him would always be with me. It was a fitting epitaph, a lasting memory.

In much the same way that his illness had forced Jon-Jo to give up his painting, I lost my ability, my passion, for gardening. Although once a fervent botanist, I could no longer enjoy the unusual flowers, walk through the scented garden or contemplate my previous fascination for poisonous plants. I should have been clearing away the debris of autumn. I hadn't the heart for it. Instead I left the plants to their own devices.

I bought a baby alarm, left it switched on beside the bed, so that I would know at once if Jon-Jo needed me. When he slept, I regularly wandered into his studio. I felt close to him there, closer than anywhere else. And, of course, the wolf drew me every time. For what seemed hours, I would gaze into his eyes and we shared our sorrow.

The district nurse visited every day, she'd learned not to comment on my husband's gradual decline, or maybe he had spoken to her. Just as I could not bear to see him suffering, I could see how it hurt him to witness my heartbreak. After my first outbursts, I managed to keep a reasonably positive outlook, so as not to distress him further.

During that first month, I thought I had resigned myself to the inevitable. Then Jon-Jo took a sudden turn for the worse. He held me gently. Kissed me. It felt as if he was saying goodbye. Then he slept peacefully. I left the bedroom, went down to the studio and sat on the floor, with my back to the wall, facing the easel. My white wolf looked down at me his eyes full of compassion, as though he understood my suffering.

I lost count of the hours I had been sitting there, the room faded into darkness; the easel was gone. Only the wolf remained. He sat, yellow eyes watching me. Then he rose. As he padded towards me, his claws scratched the floor in a calming rhythm. I could almost feel the beat of his heart; almost hear the soft panting as he sat directly in front of me. With love in my heart, I reached forward, stroked his neck. He leaned towards me, licked my face. Then he was gone. Again, it felt as if Jon-Jo was saying goodbye. The thread was broken. My thoughts tumbled out as I raced to my husband's side, frantic with worry.

Jon-Jo was still sleeping. I watched his chest rise and fall as I sobbed with relief. I knew in my heart that it was wrong to want him to continue in pain, but I couldn't part with him. I would do anything I could to save him.

That night, I had a strange dream. Candles lit one side of my husband's bed, scented candles ... rosemary. A wolf howled. It was sitting by the other side of the bed, but it was not my white wolf. This one was larger, a brownish colour with yellowish-grey markings and narrowed eyes. But there was a totally different look in his eye. A look of contempt, as though I was inferior. Sitting cross-legged, I was performing some kind of ritual, pounding herbs in a mortar. Harder and harder I worked with the pestle. But what were the herbs? I took hold of a scalpel, cut my arm, allowed the blood to drip into the mortar, and then I mixed the contents to a smooth paste. Then more blood dripped to form a drinking consistency. Seemingly without moving, I was at my husband's side. The rosemary scent wafted up in almost visible tendrils from the candles at my feet. I fed the concoction to my husband. Afterwards, I looked across at the wolf. It didn't move, but its yellow eyes still regarded me with disdain. Jon-Jo stirred. He smiled. Sat up. Flung his arms around me. I reached out to hold him... But the dream was over, I awoke suddenly to find Jon-Jo's arm, an almost flower-weight, across my body.

The following morning, I remembered the dream,

could still smell the candles. Was it a kind of prophecy? Was it the means to the miracle I needed so desperately? Before I had chance to decide, there was a knock at the door. A gnarled gypsy woman was selling wares from a huge basket.

'Cross my palm with coins and choose a gift, deary,' she said. I was about to politely decline, but she gave me a wry smile and nodded. 'I think you need some herbs, deary, don't you?'

Yes, I thought, I do need herbs. It couldn't be a coincidence, could it? I gave her some one and two pound coins and took the bunch of mixed herbs that she offered. My heart fluttered, my pulse pounded, but I knew what I must do. In readiness, I borrowed a scalpel from the studio. All day, I was on tenterhooks. Finally, darkness fell and my husband slept.

I left the bedroom door ajar. Collected a cup and my pestle and mortar from the kitchen, scooped up the bundle of herbs and the scalpel. After taking a large sticking plaster from the first aid kit, I was ready. With the images of the previous night still crystal clear, I worked carefully, pounded the herbs almost to dust. My hands shook as I contemplated the next part. I took a deep breath and sliced my forearm. The blood ran into the mortar. I mixed a smooth paste, then allowed more blood to run. It was ready. I stuck the plaster over the cut and pulled down my sleeve. My fingers trembled as I poured the precious liquid into a cup.

Jon-Jo stirred as I entered the room. He woke, and

with trusting eyes, he smiled. I offered him the cup. He drank without hesitation, handed back the cup and closed his eyes. Please, please, please, it must work. I cleared away the evidence of my activities to ensure that the district nurse would find nothing amiss when she made her usual visit in the morning.

That night I slept soundly. When I awoke, I looked eagerly at Jon-Jo. He was still asleep. A little downhearted, I dressed and went downstairs to prepare breakfast. My stomach turned somersaults as I climbed the stairs. I hesitated, prayed for the miracle I needed and opened the bedroom door. Jon-Jo smiled. Did he look a little livelier? It was difficult to say. When you want something so badly, your senses cannot be completely trusted. However, the nurse did comment that he seemed a little brighter after his relapse.

The days progressed and certainly Jon-Jo was no worse. Then during the night of the seventh day, he turned towards me, pulled me to him and kissed me. I was overjoyed. He was going to recover. I *knew* he was. Each night he was a little more amorous, a little stronger. But in the mornings, he made no comment about the night and he seemed rather weak. Perhaps, I thought, I should discourage him until he has fully regained his strength.

That night, I had a nightmare. I was hiding, squatting down, and a large brownish-grey wolf prowled in the undergrowth. He was searching, sniffing ... for me? Hardly daring to breathe, I wrapped my arms round my legs to stop my body shaking. He came closer. And closer. I held my breath. Where was my friend, the white wolf? Why didn't he come to my rescue?

Jon-Jo's arm pulled me back into reality. I tried to resist him. Tried to say that he wasn't yet strong enough. He ignored me. I'd never known him to be ... well he wasn't exactly rough, but he was not as gentle as he had always been. In the morning, he was noticeably weak. The nurse commented on it. I felt guilty. Decided I must sleep in the spare bedroom for a few nights.

The cut on my arm wasn't healing, although on the good side, it wasn't going septic either. My nightmares continued. It was always the same wolf. I had come to recognise its markings. It prowled. Howled. Each night the wolf looked for me, each night it came closer. Each night, Jon-Jo's crying out awoke me.

He seemed stronger and I decided to return to his bed. After all, being apart didn't seem to suit either of us. He had never called out when I was beside him and I was becoming very nervous of the nightmares. But they hadn't finished with me. Nor had Jon-Jo. That night, he noticed the plaster on my arm, insisted that I take it off to let him see the damage. He bent his head; I thought to kiss it better. Instead he licked the wound. It felt strange, yet I'd heard it said that the best thing for a wound [presumably if recognised treatment is unavailable] is for a dog to lick it. Well, canine saliva, human saliva, is there much difference?

The nightmare-wolf still stalked me. I quaked with terror. Happily, Jon-Jo always seemed to wake me at the crucial moment. His attentions towards me were becoming very overpowering. I felt more as if he were mating me rather than making love with me. Each morning, he was weak, obviously in pain, but made no comment.

Then, finally, came the night that the wolf smelled me out. Behind him, keeping their distance, more of his kind slinked in the shadows. But I couldn't see my white wolf anywhere. Where was he? Why had he abandoned me? This other monster was certainly on my scent. His hackles were up. Head lowered. Fangs bared. Saliva drooled as he took a step forward. Those penetrating yellow eyes never left off their stare. He crouched. Sprang.

Jon-Jo's strong arm pulled me to him. Saved me. Or so I thought. He again insisted on checking my wound, I felt the licking of a faithful hound. But the licking became the sucking of a feeding fiend. He drew back his thin lips. In his shrunken face his teeth seemingly enlarged and the muscles on his hands had contracted his thin fingers into bony claws. He was no longer my beloved Jon-Jo. That night, he had no thought for my feelings, no gentleness. I begged him to be gentle, take his time. Several times that night, he took me against my will ... he raped me.

By morning, he was very weak, yet he smiled sweetly. He obviously had no memory of the previous night. I said nothing. How could I? I knew that Jon-Jo would be mortified if he had the slightest idea of what he'd done. And, somehow I knew without question that his actions, his animal lust would become stronger.

When the nurse commented upon this weakened state, I said nothing. How could I tell her, when he didn't know what had happened? How could I betray the husband I loved with all my heart? How could I tell her what I really thought in the deepest darkest recesses of my mind?

That day, I strode out to the garden shed. I donned my gardening gloves, reached for the secateurs and garden fork. The poison garden was my destination. I must put right the wrong I had done through love and bad judgement. I went straight to the aconites, otherwise known as Monkshood or wolf-bane. All parts of the plant are deadly poison, but as it was midwinter, the only useful part of the plant was the almost turnip-shaped root. I plunged in my fork, pressed hard with my foot. The hard earth succumbed. I pulled up several of the tuberous roots, cut off and discarded the useless stems and rootlets and carried my trophies back to the house.

I washed the roots carefully before paring off the outer layer. I chopped and diced, then put the pestle to work once more. When I had ground down the pieces, I infused them in boiling water and left them stand for the remainder of the day. I was on edge all day, but Jon-

Jo was too tired to notice. He held my hand gently as I curled up beside him.

That evening, I added blackcurrant to the infusion and as much fruit sugar as it would take. With heavy legs, I climbed the stairs. Pushed the door wide open. I couldn't look Jon-Jo in the face, but I knew that I was doing the right thing, even if I paid the ultimate price myself. He took the cup, drank down every drop of the deadly brew. I kissed him goodnight, held his hand until he fell asleep. He wouldn't wake. I walked to the door. Glanced back, took one last look at the man I loved. I knew he would understand that I couldn't watch him die, knew he would understand my actions, if he was aware of the full story, of my attempt to save him.

I collected everything I had used in the preparation and took them out to the bin. Then I went into the studio. I sat, back against the wall, in front of his easel. It was such a beautiful painting. The moonlight through the large window picked out every detail of the beautiful white wolf.

I remained there, unmoving, until the moon's circuit plunged the studio into darkness. The easel was gone. But the white wolf sat there, looked at me with mournful eyes. He then padded across, licked my face ... and was gone forever.

DISPOSING OF BUNNY

He had to get rid of her, one way or another. It called for action. Now. Harry was unhappy. Plain and simple. He was due to retire next year, which was, in itself, a good thing. What he couldn't face was the prospect of being with his wife twenty-four-seven.

When he met Bunny, she was an exotic dancer, which had set him in good stead with the lads. That's when she had received her sobriquet, and it had stuck, like a scut to a rabbit. However, dating a showgirl was one thing, being married to one was quite a different matter. Naturally, he insisted that she hand in her cards, along with her tassels, and settle down to be a domestic goddess by day and his personal exotic dancer by night.

Nowadays, *moose* was more descriptive than bunny. Or yak. Y-a-k, that's better, he thought. It sounds like her. Big, drawn out, oversized. Harry sighed. He must take *some* action. Watching Bunny continually stuffing her face, getting fatter by the day, was disgusting. Over the years, it had driven them apart, in every department.

Bunny! What a ridiculous name.

He considered murder, certainly the most

permanent method. No more Bunny. Ever. Of course, he risked a new home at her Majesty's pleasure. Even in novels, there never seemed to be the perfect murder. Then there was the body. He'd read that disposing of the body was the greatest problem. She could barely get her own fat behind off the sofa these days, so how would he manage to shift her? Murder was out. Suicide was an option. Bunny's that is, not his. The snag was that Bunny was akin to a contented cow in a lush meadow. How do you convince a browsing bovine that its life isn't worth living? No. He would have to do it for her. Of course, technically, that's still murder.

What about a separation?

His thoughts strayed to the delightful Patsy. Many a time during their shared late lunches, their knees had been close. They had canoodled in corners, the corners of his mind that is, over evening meals when he'd asked her to work late. At work, their hands met when she handed a file to him. She often gave him the eye. Of course office politics, and being married, prevented him from extending their relationship. Although he knew she was willing. But separation would be like being in limbo, never free to marry someone else. Who would cook his meals and iron his shirts? Even if Patsy was a wild child, he could soon domesticate her after they were married. Separation was definitely out.

Divorce? That's a dodgy business these days. A soon-to-be ex-wife could asset strip a man in no time.

She'd even get visiting rights on his pension. It would also mean downsizing. He laughed. Pictured Bunny. Bent double with laughter when he realised that she would have to downsize too. He imagined her in a pokey flat. Guffawed at the thought of her squeezing into a bird-sized bath. On the other hand, the judge might even consider her gigantic size and declare that she should have the larger share.

He remembered all the long hours he had worked to provide for his bride. The four-bed house he'd hardly seen in the early years. No children had blessed their marriage. Bunny took to eating and he... Harry continued working, with occasional extracurricular overtime. Years ago, he had moved into a separate bedroom. Yes, he decided, it had its drawbacks, but divorce was the only solution.

He thought of little else during that day. Nobody noticed. Over the years, he had learned to delegate. Nobody questioned. Why should they? This was good old hardworking Harry. He never slacked. Patsy's smile seemed more inviting than usual. Yes, he thought, Patsy is the girl for me. On the train home, his stomach tied itself in knots. He hoped his fellow travellers couldn't smell his nerves turning to liquid and resisted the urge to have a quick sniff at his armpits.

When he opened the door, the aroma of a casserole wafted from the kitchen, excited his taste buds. Bunny *was* a good cook. She placed two brimming plates on the table, turned back for the extra tureen of potatoes and vegetables. He ate without looking up. There was no need. He knew she would scrape the tureen clean without any help from him. She ate like a starving navvy. Jam roly-poly followed, with lashing of thick creamy custard.

'Bunny,' he said later that evening. 'We hardly spend any time together. I've been thinking about retirement. How will it be?'

She looked at him, raised an eyebrow. 'How will what be?'

'Us,' he said. 'You know. How will we get on? I'll be under your feet all day. You wouldn't like that, would you?'

'What are you leading up to?'

'Well ... that is ... I think we should get a divorce.'

'Good idea!'

'You what!' Harry's jaw dropped. 'You mean ... you *want* a divorce?'

'Why not? Like you said, we hardly spend any time together. With my share of everything, I could set myself up. Probably be a lot happier too.'

'Right,' Harry said, his ego deflated. He had expected tears, cries of, "please don't leave me, I need you", not this easy acquiescence. 'Well... yes ... that's settled then. I'll see a solicitor tomorrow.'

That night, Harry barely slept. He couldn't believe it had been so easy. Then doubts started to creep in. Why was she so amiable? What was she hiding? He almost choked as the next thought crossed his mind.

She can't have! She's never met somebody else? No. Who would look at her twice?

At breakfast, he faced her. 'Have you met somebody else?'

'No,' she said. 'Whatever gave you that idea?'

'You were that quick to agree to a divorce ... as though you wanted to be rid of me.'

'You obviously aren't happy,' Bunny said, 'or you wouldn't have mentioned divorce. I don't like our present lifestyle either.'

He felt betrayed. 'I see.'

'Last night,' she said, 'I was awake most of the night, thinking. We ought to put the house up for sale straight away. Ask a reasonable price and somebody will probably snap it up. Spring *is* the best time to sell.'

'Right.'

'Sharing out the furniture should be easy,' she said. 'There's plenty for us both.'

'You *have* been planning.'

Bunny looked him straight in the face. 'Like I said, I was awake all night. Couldn't sleep. The shock of it all, I suppose.'

Shock! Never mind shock. He was numb. It took the whole of his commute before he fully grasped that he'd got everything he wanted without even a scuffle, let alone a fight. He arrived at work feeling quite cheerful. During an extended lunchtime, he instigated divorce proceedings and put the house on the market.

Later that day, Patsy walked into his office with the

last of the files. He motioned to a corner of his desk.

'Put them there will you.' He smiled at her. 'Sorry, I kept you late again. How about something to eat? We could go to that little bistro on James Street.'

'That would be lovely, Harry. Thanks.'

He rubbed his hands when she left the office. This is going to be the start of the rest of my life, he thought.

At the bistro, Harry chose a small corner table. He wanted to tell her his good news straightway. However, saying you're getting divorced isn't something you can just blurt out to a girl; you have to work the conversation round to it. Every time he thought he had it nailed, she chimed in with something about the office, or the food.

Bunny's intuition regarding the house was correct. They had kept the price reasonable and a family offered the asking price within three days. Harry had never felt so light hearted. Life was hotting up.

A week later, Bunny made her announcement. 'I've found a house that will suit me fine. It's quite close to town, and has a small garden.'

Harry decided to rent first. He wanted Patsy at least to feel that she had a say about where they should live.

Bunny moved into her house. She didn't invite him over, which he thought was rather mean spirited of her. It didn't give him chance to decline due to his burgeoning social life. Instead, she rang him, said that she preferred a clean break.

The months passed. He'd seen neither hide nor scut

of Bunny. Finally, the decree absolute was granted. He was free to make his play for Patsy. I'll treat myself to a few fashionable clothes, he thought. Show her I can cut it with the youngsters.

After a little prodding and a twenty pound note slipped into each eager hand, several young assistants in the trendiest shops gave their advice. Grinning like an old tomcat going on the tiles, he clung to the designer carrier bags. He hesitated on the pavement. Glanced across the road. He gasped. Dropped a couple of packages. It couldn't be! It was. There was Patsy, in a clinch with a young lad. Forget clinch! The lad was practically *eating* her. And her arms were all over him like an octopus devouring its prey.

On Monday morning the general office was in uproar. He looked up. Everyone was round Patsy's desk. But where was she? Was she okay? He jumped up. Stepped out of his office. The crowd parted. Patsy stood up, walked towards him.

She waved an engagement ring under his nose.

'Look, Harry, isn't it lovely? I'm getting married. We bought the ring on Saturday.'

Harry gulped. Hoped the staff took his reaction as surprise. 'Very nice indeed, Patsy,' he said. 'Congratulations.'

He escaped back into his office. How could she? She'd led him on. He was devastated. Patsy had been his. All morning, he pondered the situation. Finally realised the truth. He now saw those meals with her for what they really were. Patsy obviously accepted her boss's invitation to go for something to eat as a compensation for working late. Nothing more.

After work, he walked back to his flat. Why, he mused, doesn't life tell you what it has in store for you? At least with Bunny, I had a good meal cooked for me. He was deep in self-pity. Almost collided with a couple walking, arm-in-arm, towards him.

'Harry!'

Harry looked up. Peered closer.

'Surely you recognise me,' Bunny said. 'This is Clive. We met at Weight Watchers. He's a fitness instructor and has been encouraging me, helping me to lose a few pounds. We're getting married next month.'

He stared. She was a shadow of the woman she had been. All the excess fat was gone. Bunny was nicely rounded, very attractive. Her face reminded him of the girl he had married. She hardly looked any older. God almighty, he thought, she's a bunny girl again! And, more to the point, she'd got herself a young buck.

'Sorry, I was miles away,' Harry said. His stomach lurched, tried to hold on to its last meal. 'Er ... congratulations! Sorry, must dash, I'm meeting someone.'

'Nice to meet you,' Clive said.

Harry nodded. He walked on. Desolate. Why couldn't she have done that for me, he thought. I would have paid for her to go to Weight Watchers. I would have encouraged her. I would have ... She only had to ask. Why didn't she just ask?

NINE LIVES

The last rays of the weak afternoon sun filtered through the shrubbery, but did nothing to alleviate the freezing daytime temperatures. As Felix drove along the quiet road he was relaxed, contented, believed that life at thirty was all it should be. He had a good job, a good car and a varied collection of good-time girls. As though in disagreement, there was a rattle of laughter from behind him. Instinctively, he turned round to confirm that the back seat was vacant. In those few moments he lost concentration. The car hit black ice. Veered alarmingly. He tried to regain control, but the tyres, in collusion with the ice, had a mind of their own and were unresponsive to his manoeuvring. The car hit the raised verge, flipped in the air and ... he blacked out.

When Felix Sylvester started to regain consciousness, everything appeared to be white and his befuddled brain told him he was in heaven, with the angels. As his senses became fully operational, he realised that the front airbag was squashing into the top half of his face. He sat upright. Took in a few gulps of air. Felt his arms. Wriggled his toes. Everything *was* white ... everything that is, except the pitch-blackness that peered in through the large numerals written on the thickly frosted windscreen: 1 – 8. That was it! 1 – 8! Who the devil would write on the window, he thought. Surely if somebody had been there, they would have tried to get him out ... at least opened the door to see if he was alive. Another outburst of laughter caused a spidery prickle on the back of his neck and reminded him about the cause of the crash.

A growing shaft of light piercing the windscreen numerals made him look at its source. A cloud had drifted, shown the full moon in all its naked glory. It now provided the light he needed to escape his predicament and guide him home. He angled the rear-view mirror, studied his face, and sighed with relief to find that it was unmarked. Then he noticed his gingery jowls. With a grin, he accepted that they were now pushing designer stubble to the limit; maybe he'd set a new fashion. But the amount of growth concerned him. With frozen fingers he tugged at his sleeve; his watch showed that he had been there for about seven hours. He struggled to unfasten his seat belt, which together with the front and side airbags had no doubt saved him from serious injury and given him some protection from the freezing cold that seeped in through the shattered side windows.

Felix disentangled himself from the air bags and tried unsuccessfully to open the door. Sitting sideways, he kicked the door several times before it begrudgingly opened. The biting cold gripped him. Then he gave a low whistle as he studied the remains of his car. Since, from the inside, the front end had seemed relatively intact, he had assumed that the car had merely flipped once and settled back on its wheels. However, seen from *outside*, it looked as if some enraged navvy had steam-rollered the rear end. He stuck his head back inside, looked towards the back, except that there was hardly any back seat visible. Then he saw for the first time that the front was also missing a good portion of its headroom. It was unbelievable. He sniggered and thought that there was, at least in this case, a definite advantage of being on the short side, otherwise his body could have lost a vital component ... its head. The car must have rolled several times and most probably struck some of the boulders that littered the slope down which his car had tried out its off-road capabilities.

He whistled again. Being alive, although he was thankful, was something that puzzled him. How had he managed to escape from that mangled motor without permanent damage, without a bruise? He didn't even have the slightest soreness from where the seat belts must have dug in. Luck had certainly been on his side, but it then promptly deserted him when he felt for his mobile. He cursed. Remembered that the phone was sitting on his table ... charging its batteries. He flapped his arms about, tried to restore some warmth, but it was a losing battle. The icy mantle of hypothermia was beginning to claim him, envelop him. It set his teeth chattering and he was sure he had frostbite in his fingers, possibly in his toes too.

He knew that some serious exercise was his only option; it would keep him warm and lead him back to the road, although it was going to be a hard climb. He sighed. It was probably only a slight incline to most, but to someone whose only past experience was climbing the stairs and into bed, preferably with female accompaniment, this would be his Everest. At least, he thought, as he climbed, his new trainers had a good grip, even if he could no longer feel his feet, but he still needed to use his bare, frozen hands to help him clamber to the top.

Gasping for breath, but feeling some warmth creeping into his bones, he reached the verge. He looked in both directions; the landscape was totally devoid of buildings. Ground frost coated the road, except for a couple of sets of wheel tracks. Then he saw what he first assumed to be skid marks. They weren't! The joker that had written on his windscreen had also been playing silly devils on the road. He had scraped away the frost to read 2 – 7. Felix swore heartily at the unknown person who'd thought it clever to carve cryptic messages, yet could have left him to die. He was too tired to think. It was three-thirty, far too early for commuter traffic, too late for errant partygoers. So, he had no choice. He would have to travel under his own steam. Of course, he reflected, it would be handy to have some ... steam, that is. At present he was beginning to resemble an ice sculpture and did not intend to become the finished article. In an effort to gain more warmth, he set off at a slow jog and somehow managed to maintain the pace until he reached home.

Wearily, he climbed the stairs to his second floor flat and then rested to take a few gulps of air and let his heart rate normalise. He unlocked the door. Clicked on the light. The single bare light bulb glared over part of the large bed-sit while leaving the rest in darkness. He kicked the door shut. Still fully dressed, he flopped onto the bed, pulled over the duvet and flicked off the light.

When he awoke, he shivered, chilled to the bone. He wriggled out of bed, reached for the box of matches to light the paltry gas fire. Before he could even take out the match, a sudden coughing fit overcame him, nearly choked him. Gas! He stumbled to the window. Pushed it open and gulped in a lungful of fresh air, then several more. Once recovered, he left the window open and returned to the gas fire. The valve was partly open. He closed it, but wondered how that could have happened. If, he reasoned, he'd left the gas turned on, but unlit, when he went out, or even mistakenly turned it on in the early hours then ... well, he thought, he wouldn't have woken up at all. Ever.

With a glance at the clock, he realised he'd missed a whole day and now it was almost dark again. He was in sore need of warmth. As he wrapped the duvet round his shoulders his stomach grumbled, reminded him that its furnace was also in need of replenishment. That previously heard weird laughter now crackled round the room before it came to rest as a sting on the back of his neck. He ignored it. The shock of the accident was obviously affecting him. He sniffed. The air smelt clear, so he went back to the window, but someone had written on the steamed-up glass: 3 – 6. He looked down to the pavement. Certainly nobody had climbed up to his window; there was no drainpipe, trellis or anything else to assist a would-be climber. Even the straggle of ivy only made it over the first dozen or so bricks.

He closed the window, drew the curtains and flicked on the light. As he looked through the fridge for something to eat, he heard that obscene laughter again. It was coming from the far corner. That corner was a particular bugbear. In it was the only cupboard, more of a walk-in closet. It was where he kept his clothes and he needed to bring them over to the light before he could tell what he was holding, otherwise there would have been some weird combinations.

'All right, the joke's over,' he said to whoever was hiding in the corner. 'Come on out.'

Nothing happened.

'I know you're there. Come on out. Let's see you face to face.'

There was a muffled sound from the corner, then a strange voice. 'Eventually, you and every other person will see me, face to face, but you will not like what you see.'

'Stop stalking me! And what's all this 1 - 8 ... 2 - 7 ... 3 - 6 about? Who are you?'

'I am Death. I stalk every human being until their allotted time is come.'

Felix was beginning to think that he must have concussion from the crash. But he couldn't resist continuing this strange conversation. 'Don't talk rot! I've never heard of anybody, even the loonies, saying that they can see Death stalking them.'

'Of course not! Each person has only one life. Therefore nobody knows I am stalking him. You are different.'

'Oh, yes? How's that, then?'

'You must work that out for yourself. Goodbye, Felix ... for now.'

The fridge door was still open. He pulled out a piece of cheese, cut off the mouldy edges and sliced it between some bread and butter. Something hot and spicy would have been more satisfying, but at least he had food and now his body was beginning to warm. He started to think about what Death had said. One thing for sure, he couldn't tell anybody about what was happening, they'd have him certified. So, what was it about? Although he'd had three lucky escapes from Death, there was nothing odd about that as people have narrow escapes every day. And besides, his name, Felix, meant "good luck". Was that it? Was it something to do with his name?

He remembered when some bright kid at school

had learned that *felis sylvestris* was the Latin name for a wild cat and it was too close to his name for the soubriquet not to stick. He became "Wild Cat", then "Top Cat" and later "Ginger Tom". He laughed. He'd certainly lived up to the last, as there'd been innumerable and very successful nights out on the tiles. They always said that ginger-haired men don't have as much appeal to women ... well, he'd proved that one wrong. Even now, fifteen years after leaving school, he was still fit. In his prime in fact, and he could have any girl he wanted.

Suddenly, he made sense of it all. It was 1 - 8 after his accident. Was the 2 - 7 because he had miraculously survived hours in the freezing cold? Then it was 3 - 6 when a potential gas explosion could have blown him, and the whole building, sky-high. It added up to one thing. Somehow, he had acquired a cat's nine lives. He laughed. Nine lives! And it sounded as if this Death chap had his nose put right out of joint about it. But I've got him sussed out, Felix thought, so I reckon I've got the edge. He resolved to be extra careful not to fall into any traps.

The next morning, while the snails were sorting out his car insurance, Felix walked to the bus station. Luck was on his side. There was an empty seat, or at least about a third of a seat. The large woman overflowing onto his side was certainly getting value for her ticket. But, he thought, a third of a seat is better than standing. The person across the aisle stood up to get off the bus, left behind a neatly folded newspaper. Felix grabbed the seat and pocketed the paper.

Only on his return journey did he remember the discarded newspaper, but there was no chance to read it on the crowded bus. When he did settle down at home, he saw that somebody, obviously not a very bright bean, had started the crossword. Started was right, he'd only done 3 across: Death in Venice. He felt that familiar prickle on the back of his neck. So, he thought, you're at it again, are you? Well, up yours! I'm not going to Venice. And that's certain ... because my passport's out of date.

He laughed. 'Let's see you beat that one!'

The next morning, Saturday, Felix realised that he would have to go to the shops on foot. What a drudge! In his mind, he worked out the quickest route and set off. As he turned a corner, with the small supermarket in view, there was a sudden cry from above.

Felix looked up. Saw something massive falling his way. He jumped. Dodged the missile.

'Sorry about that, mate,' said the grinning idiot who clambered down the ladder. 'The chain gave way.'

Felix shot him a poison stare. Then looked at the battered board lying near his feet. The board was advertising a closing down sale, which it claimed was from the 4th – 5th of the next month. Well, he smirked, there may be some bargains later, but something had already come down. Then the four and the five stood out as if in 3D. Immediately, the sharp retort he had in mind dissolved, even so, he gave the culprit another glare before he walked off. As he crossed the road, he noticed the sign: *Venice Avenue*. It's surprising what you miss, or ignore, when you're driving, he thought. Then the full weight of the situation dawned on him. The crafty old sod! He *knew* I would have to come here, if I wanted to eat. Presumably Death didn't ... eat that is ... but he must have stalked enough humans to know that we do need food on a regular basis.

Struggling outside with his shopping bulging in several carrier bags, he knew one thing for sure. Shopping was a mug's game, especially if you didn't have a car. It set him wondering about his several current girlfriends. Not that he expected something for nothing, of course. The girl of his choice would have his full attentions in the bedroom, well at least on the pull out-sofa bed. In return she would be in charge of the kitchen area. She could shop and cook, maybe do a bit of ironing too. Any of the girls would be bound to jump at the chance, they wouldn't be able to resist.

With his mind fully occupied deciding which lucky girl he would have, he stepped out into the road. There was a screech of brakes as a scarlet E-type thrust its bonnet where it had no right to be. Fortunately, his trousers, although only two centimetres from the classic status symbol, were unscathed. His shopping wasn't so lucky. As he bent to retrieve his purchases, he stared at the car and its occupant. From the elderly driver's equally red face and gesticulations the man was extending his vocabulary. Then, with a high-powered rev, he drove off. The number plate drew Felix's attention: *LOVER 54*. It was obviously an attempt at a personalised plate.

Felix sniggered, muttered: 'He wishes.'

However, when read in conjunction with the two fixing screws, it gave a whole new meaning: L-OVER 5-4. Felix laughed out loud. Stupid pillock, he thought, over 70 might be more like it. Then the smile vanished. Instead, a nasty feeling jabbed at the back of his neck, caused him to scurry home as fast as his shopping would allow.

Panting from the unaccustomed exercise, he plonked the carriers down and grabbed a can of lager. He sprawled out on the sofa. Decided that things were getting out of hand, but from past experience he would have no chance to say his piece until after dark. In the meantime, he put the shopping away and relaxed for the rest of the day.

Darkness was asserting itself when Felix heard the first sound from the darkened corner.

'Right, you,' he said, before Death had a chance to speak. 'You're not playing fair. So, okay, I may be missing two feet and be devoid of retractable claws, but, according to you, I have the same nine lives that a cat has. Right?'

There was a slight shuffle from the corner.

'Too ashamed to speak, that's it, isn't it? You're

playing dirty. No cat loses five of its lives in three days. Fact! Right? So what've you got to say about that then?'

'I do not, as you call it, "play dirty",' Death said. 'I follow strict rules. If you break the rules, you pay the consequences.'

'What rules? You haven't said anything about any rules.'

'Of course not. Where would the point of that be?'

'How can we follow what's going on if we don't know the rules?'

Again, there was that awful rattling laugh from the corner and it was beginning to annoy him, but he kept his cool.

'No human knows the rules,' Death said, 'that's the whole point of life. Nobody knows when I will come visiting.'

Felix had no answer to that, but to him, it didn't seem at all fair. 'Does that mean, then, that I could lose my remaining four lives in a few days?'

'Are you trying to catch me out? You *could* lose all your remaining lives in *one* day, even in one hour. On the other hand, you may live to be a very old man.'

He sensed that Death had gone, without being of much help. Well, he thought as he started cooking spaghetti Bolognese for his dinner, I'm safe for the rest of today and tomorrow. The girls can have a night off, too. As I won't be going out, I'll make sure that the gas fire is lit, or securely switched off. He tipped half the pan load onto a plate, left the remainder on the stove.

Gas turned off! The rest of the evening was uneventful, and after retiring to bed in the small hours, he had a good night's sleep.

On Sunday morning, or rather around midday, he got up. Lit the fire. Several cups of coffee later, he felt at a bit of a loss. Decided a couple of slices of toast and marmalade would go down well. Everything seemed strange. Empty. He was accustomed to some girl staying over from the night before, sharing his Sunday.

As time dragged itself round to six, he reached for the pan of leftover spaghetti Bolognese. He dug a spoon in. Released the solid mass from the base of the pan. The pan swivelled in his hand, shed into contents on the floor. He cursed. Then shrugged his shoulders and bent down to retrieve his dinner. When he returned it to the work surface, he realised it had aged. Rapidly! It now had whiskers, and fluff and heaven knows what else firmly embedded. He chucked the lot in the waste bin.

With sudden realisation, he laughed. 'That's one to me. I could have eaten that lot and maybe choked on all that muck.'

'I think you will find,' Death said, 'that it is one more to me.'

'You what?'

'You left the food out, in a very warm room, causing the meat to go off. You could have died of food poisoning. The score is 6 – 3. You are not playing the game very well, are you?'

Game! He thinks it's a game? Well, I'm not playing his games, Felix thought, and I'll soon put a stop to his fun. Then the truth of the situation came to him. The only way he could prepare to cheat Death was in Death's absence. Which meant, since it was still dark when he left for work and the last gasp of twilight when he returned, he would have to survive until Saturday. Death never visited his flat in the daylight, when there was no dark corner in which to hide, so, the dark corner was the key. He had a week to make a foolproof plan.

He barely slept that night as there was so much going on in his mind. Then he had a nightmare – about Death, naturally.

Next morning, he was late for the bus, saw it approaching the stop and ran full pelt. It slowed slightly, as if to taunt him, then started to accelerate. He took a flying leap and grabbed the rail. The conductor/driver gave him a dirty look, which Felix returned. The mean so-and-so could have waited for me, he thought. He had to stand for the whole journey and was cursing silently when the bus eventually pulled into his stop. Of course, since it wasn't his custom to travel by bus, he hadn't known that this particular bus had changed its route number. He glanced at the indicator: 72. However, some bird had thought fit to comment on the bus service and had left its calling card between the two digits. Things were getting desperate.

For the rest of week, he played it by the book. No late nights, ergo, no late mornings and no running for the bus. He had more or less formulated a plan and on Friday night went to make the necessary purchases.

The chap next to him must have missed a few rungs on the evolutionary ladder, because he swung up the metal framework of the shelving, agile as a monkey, and reached for a four-litre can of paint. He got his paint. And reached the floor in safety. Lucky sod! Unfortunately, he also released several other large cans. They teetered on the edge, swayed dangerously. Gravity won. Felix jumped clear as they hit the floor, but they hadn't finished with him. One can burst open, sent a cascade of yellow paint to decorate the left leg of his jeans. He didn't need to see the score. He knew that he was back to being a mere mortal with only the one life.

On Saturday morning, he was up at the crack of dawn, which being winter, was about 9.30. He made coffee and quickly set to work. First he took the lid off his tin of gloss paint. He'd chosen black. Under the circumstances, it seemed to be the most appropriate colour. He drilled a hole in the side, near the top, and threaded string through before knotting it securely. After tapping the ceiling, he found a joist. It wouldn't do to have the lot fall on his head, not at this crucial time. He screwed in the largest hook he had been able to buy. Then he tied a short length of cord to the hook and to the paint can's handle. The next bit was trickier.

He needed to fasten the string that dangled from the side of the can through a serious of hooks. After doing that, he gently pulled the string, just a fraction. The can moved.

Satisfied, he stood back. With a smirk, he nodded at his own ingenuity. Then he picked up a blanket, which may have started out as any colour, but was now predominantly grey, and as rough as a tramp's beard. Strategically, he placed it at the ready, together with a sturdy clothesline. He almost forgot the bolts. He'd purchased the strongest available and now screwed them to the bottom, middle and top of the closet door. Lastly, he screwed a spotlight on the wall, turned it to face the corner. Then he added more cord to the light's pull switch. He was ready.

Death followed dusk into his flat. Felix stood. His palms were wet and clammy. His heart thumped in an alarming manner. He tugged at the end of the string. Heard the paint splatter. He ran forward. Yanked the pull switch. Threw the blanket over the now visible black shape in the corner. The gloss paint sucked at the blanket. Quick as a flash Felix wound the clothes line round Death. He knotted the cord. Then, just for luck, tied more knots. He bundled Death into the closet. Shut the door and threw the bolts. He then stuffed a sheet into the crevice beneath the door. The gap was less than a quarter of an inch, but when you're dealing with Death, you never know what tricks he has up his sleeve, or wherever Death keeps his tricks.

Felix could have danced with joy. He was safe. Safe and secure, thanks to his cleverness.

All went well for a few days. Then one subject dominated the news. The headlines screamed: *"Man survives horrific accident"*. What's unusual in that, Felix thought. People survive all sorts of things. It reminded him of his own miraculous escape, it also made him wonder if there was another guy with nine lives. But then, when he read further, he found it was very unsettling. Apparently this chap had compound fractures of both legs, both arms and his ribs. On top of that, several vertebrae were compacted and his spinal cord severed. You'd think that was enough ... but it wasn't, he also had third-degree burns over most of his body. The medical profession were astounded that the man was still alive. They stated that such extensive burns would normally be sufficient to kill the victim. The report finished by saying that the man was in a coma. Well, Felix thought with a sigh, that's a relief!

Then he realised that this situation was only the start. With Death having joined the ranks of the unemployed, there could be no *fatal* accidents, no *terminal* diseases. Everybody would go on living. Nobody would ever die. People would be injured, or ill, and go from bad to worse, to... It would be a living hell on earth. The hospitals wouldn't be able to cope. Nobody would understand what was happening. Except Felix. He knew. He had trapped Death in his closet.

He couldn't bear the thought of the screaming, the suffering. Yet, he couldn't tell anybody. Couldn't seek help. This was something he had to face alone. He would have to make profuse apologies to Death and promise that he wouldn't try anything ever again for as long as he lived. He meant it too.

He unbolted the closet. Opened the door. Unwound the clothesline that bound Death. With trembling hands, he lifted the blanket. He tried not to look at his captive, but Death had him in his grip. Felix saw the writing on the wall, and he knew that Death had almost finished his game. The game he played with everyone, the playing time of which he extended until it reached the allotted hour. The writing was faint, barely legible, but growing clearer. 9 – 0! Then Death made him turn. Further. Further. Until Felix was facing Death, staring him straight in the face.

TO PEE, OR NOT TO PEE

Oak moved to the head of the table. 'In accordance with my standing in society, I trust everyone will agree that I take the chair.'

'Not so fast, mate,' Grass said. He hated the way those posh types treated everybody else like dirt. 'Why should you be in charge?'

There was a sharp intake of breath from Oak. 'My dear fellow, I am the definitive symbol of British plant life. My forebears provided the ships for Henry VIII. I can trace my ancestry back to the eighth century. I am Britain personified.'

'Rubbish!' Grass stood his ground, determined to show that he had some knowledge too. 'What a load of cobblers! Most of the grasses were here first. You've only got to go and listen to that Darwin chap ... he'll tell you...'

Trying to make the peace, bring some order to the proceedings, Chrysanthemum leapt to his feet.

'Perhaps we should take a vote.'

There were nods all round and Chrysanthemum distributed the voting papers. They counted the votes. And ... Oak resumed his place at the head of the table. While Grass, though temporarily sidelined, was planning a comeback. Planning not only to make his views heard, but also to have them adopted. Those humans didn't keep referring to grass roots for nothing, he thought.

'As I was about to say, we must make a stand to establish our rights.' The door squeaked open. Oak glanced up. Looked at the interloper. 'And whom, may I ask, am I addressing? You do not appear to be listed.'

'I had no representation, so I came alone. I am Japanese Knot.'

'Like as hell you are,' Grass said. 'You're Japanese Knot*weed*. One of them illegals. One of them we've being trying to get rid of.'

Japanese Knot coiled in embarrassment. 'I must disagree. And I have tried my best to integrate into society. No one consulted my forebears regarding their emigration. Eminent plant collectors brought them here because they recognised their potential as an attractive addition to the gardens of England.'

'Rubbish! You're just a common weed!'

'Grass! That's enough,' Oak said. 'We will not stand for speciesism. Everyone will either address a member by his botanical name or his ordinary name. Derogatory terms are unacceptable ... we will punish their usage. Is that understood?'

Grass flexed his sap, muttered under his breath.

Oak scanned the room. Seemed satisfied that there would be no more outbreaks of bad manners. 'Please be seated, Japanese Knot, or would you prefer to be addressed by your botanical name to avoid further controversy?' Knot nodded. 'You're welcome, *Polygonum.* Since our ancestors received you into this country, we are happy for you to stay in our midst. Perhaps, for the time being at least, you may remain in a group of your own.'

There were numerous nods and calls of approval. But they didn't fool Grass. He knew that the others felt as he did, that nobody wanted Knotweed in *their* group.

'My first task is to announce the various groups to which we have all been allocated.

Group 1: I represent all the trees, with the exception of fruit trees.

Group 2: Orchid is leader of all the hothouse plants, not to include the wild orchids to which I will refer later.

Group 3: Daffodil leads bulbs, corms, rhizomes and other tuberous plants, except root vegetables.

Group 4: Chrysanthemum symbolizes perennial plants, including herbs.

Group 5: Wallflower was the choice of the annuals and biennials.

Group 6: Rose personifies the shrubs and bushes.

Group 7: Thistle represents wild flowers, to include the wild orchid population.

Group 8: Potato heads the vegetable division.

Group 9: Apple speaks for the fruits, to include fruit trees, bushes and soft fruits.

Group 10: Old Man's Beard leads the climbers and ramblers.

Group 11: Grass represents all the varieties of grass, cereals and bamboos.

I believe that covers everybody.'

Thanks for that reminder, thought Grass. 'I wish to object. Why should you classify bamboos with the grass community? They're more like trees ... or else immigrants, like *Polygonum*.'

'He has a point,' said Thistle. 'I cannae see why I should speak for yon bonny wee flowers. They dinna have the same problems.'

A darker hue blushed Rose's petals as she stood up.

'They are of course correct. The Butterfly Bush is in my group, and it *is* a lovely name, but she has a terrible reputation. She sprouts up everywhere at the drop of a seedcase. I have even seen her rooted in a chimney pot. I shouldn't be expected to represent such promiscuous behaviour.'

Oak shook his head. Stood up. Motioned everybody else to sit. 'That is enough! We are here today for a particular matter. That is to fight for the rights of *all* plants. I concede that the groups are, maybe, not ideal...' There was an undercurrent of murmurs, a couple of raps on the table. 'However ... that is not the issue. Boundary changes can be discussed at a future date.'

'Excuse me,' a small voice piped up. 'I still do not have a group.'

'My apologies, *Polygonum,*' Oak said. 'Let me see ... you will be Group 12.'

'Aye, ye say there'll be a discussion. But do we have ye word on it? I need assurances tae take back to my ain group. Nettles, in particular, are gey belligerent.'

Oak sighed. 'Yes, you have my word. Now may we please continue, or else this will turn into an all night sitting.'

Everybody settled down, all eyes on Oak.

'We will proceed in group order...'

'He's at it again! It's always the toffs that come first,' Grass said. What about the rest of us? We...'

'Very well. We will take reverse order,' Oak said.

Grass smirked. A small victory, but everything counts. Get yourself noticed, that's the motto, get yourself noticed. Let them know that they can't trample on the little people.'

'Now, let me see ... ah, yes...' Oak sighed. Then gave a forced smile in the direction of the newcomer to the talks. 'Group 12, what are your grievances?'

Polygonum clearly felt uneasy within the spotlight. 'I ... that is *we* are treated with total contempt...'

'Quite right, too,' Grass said. 'I've heard the humans say that once you're in, you're the Devil's own job to get rid of.'

'Grass! Remember that *Polygonum* is one of us. Kindly show more restraint, and respect.' Oak turned to the leader of group 12. 'What is your specific complaint?'

'They use ... weed-killer.' *Polygonum* looked round. 'Yes, that's right. Those are the very words they use. Even the terminology is a violation of our rights. It's technical term is herbicide, and I think the very word should be expunged and its use should be banned.'

'Aye, and here's another thing,' Thistle said. 'When it doesnae kill a plant, there's terrible disfigurement. Ban yon squirty bottles and the humans' machinery that flings out death far and wide, and yon wee sharp tools that pickle out what's left of our roots.'

Oak seemed rather disinterested, but then, Grass thought, he would, wouldn't he? That weed-killer isn't for trees.

'We will vote on the abolition of weed-killer as a violation of our rights to life and dignity. Those in favour.' Oak looked round. 'Clause one ... carried unanimously.'

'We proceed to group 11,' Oak said.

Grass didn't need to hear more. He stood up.

'Brothers and sisters! It's a universally accepted fact that the world would collapse without grass. Humans would starve without cereals.'

'Aye, a man cannae survive if he doesnae get his oats.'

'Thank you, Thistle,' Grass said. 'Men eat cereals, and feed them *and* grass to their animals. Yet how do humans treat us? It's bad enough when they let their animals pee on us, but how would you feel to get a load of sh ... sorry sisters ... a load of poo plopping on your head?'

Thistle laughed. 'Sorry, laddie. I dinna mean no disrespect. I was bringing to mind the wee doggies trying to poop on yon nettles or my wee thistle cousins.'

Grass was unsure whether he was receiving support or not. 'We need a total ban on all domestic animals being let loose. That's what we need. Let's see if they like the stink in their own back yard.'

There were mumbles of agreement, several nods of heads.

Oak rapped on the table. 'You do have a point, Grass. However, we must address this issue with care. If we want our Bill to go through, we must ensure that the humans will not shoot down any of its clauses. What about the natural animals? Do they not, er, do they not defecate upon your kind?'

'Of course they do. But that's nature. Besides it's not just about hygiene and manners. It's about stink. Wild animal sh ... stuff don't stink. Domestic animal stuff does ... specially cows. You'd know it if you ever got plopped on from a height.'

'He's right,' Thistle said. 'Have ye no smelled the heathers? Deer, rabbits and the like graze *and* defecate and there's no any stink.'

Oak began to look jaded. Grass smirked. That'll teach the pompous sod to demand to be chairman. He's no idea how to do the job. No idea how to lead.

'Clause 2 carried,' Oak said. 'Now we have...'

'Hang on! Give as a chance, I haven't done yet.'

Grass stood up to establish his current authority. 'There's mowing...'

Oak drummed the table. 'We cannot accept general moans...'

'Get your bark re-corked! I said, *"mowing"*. Honestly, some folk ... they cut you short at the drop of a leaf. Now, about *mowing*. I'm as amiable as the next guy; I don't mind the odd haircut. But we have to make a stand against them chopping us to the ground. And what's it for? All those sports activities the humans bash on about, and for that they slash us down to the roots, it's just not cricket.'

'Aye, he's right. Humans have slashed down many a thistle in his prime, the nettles, too. If we chopped yon humans off by their ankles, and they wouldnae like it. They wouldnae like it at all.'

Oak resumed control. 'Yes, I must concede that many of my kind are bole-axed. Some survive ... others just pine away. Clause 3 carried?'

Everyone nodded and grass, fully vindicated, sat down.

There was a sigh from Oak. 'Group 10 ... that's you, Old Man's Beard.'

'I may have a few creaky joints, but I object to you using ageist remarks. I'd prefer it if you called me Traveller's Joy since it suits my personality better. We're an underrated group and often maligned ... we are certainly not rampant.'

Grass snorted. 'You speak for yourself, mate. What

about that Russian Vine, it's not called Mile-a-Minute for nothing.'

Traveller's Joy blushed. 'Every group has its black sheep. The points I wish to make have already been covered, that is herbicide and cutting to the ground.'

'Thank you, Traveller's Joy,' Oak said as he looked pointedly at Grass. 'We move on to Group 9. Your comments, Apple.'

Apple stood up, gathered her ample skirts about her, and gave everyone a winning smile, as her already rosy cheeks blushed scarlet. 'Our needs are simple, my dears. We bear fruit and launch our offspring into the world. But there are fatalities.' She wiped away a tear. 'Some of our children are mutilated by the insects, others fall prey to animals. That is nature. So, painful as it is, it has to be borne. But the humans strip us bare. They take every last child, every one. It's inhumane. It's ... it's...'

'There, there, Apple, don't take on so.' Oak extended a branch of friendship towards the weeping mother. 'This is certainly grounds for Clause 4. No need for a show of hands.'

Apple resumed her seat, stifled her sobs.

Oak granted her a moment's respect, then continued. 'Group 8, what have you to say, Potato?'

'Much the same as Ma Apple, guv. Our ancestors were happy enough, but all that's gone. Like she said, they strip us bare. What's more, they desiccate or uproot us. Call it cultivation, they do. Mutilation, that's what it is, mutilation and annhi... annihi'

Oak smiled. 'Yes, we comprehend your meaning, Potato. So that's Clause 5, no desiccating, uprooting or annihilation. Wait a moment! The humans will claim that they need food, so let's not be hasty. Should we say no desiccating, and only moderate uprooting for immediate consumption?'

'If you say so, guv,' Potato said. 'It's always the farming community that bears the burden. Always us who have to make sacrifices.'

Thistle stood up. 'Group 7 is next – that's me. Like the other folk, we dinnae want herbicides and chopping down.' He puffed out his thistledown. 'But we deserve special treatment. The thistle is a national emblem. *And* it's on the royal regalia, approved by the Queen herself.'

'We *all* have some royal connection.' Oak stood tall. 'Charles the First chose one of *my* ancestors to hide in.'

'Lay off! If anybody can claim royal connection, it's me,' said Grass. 'There isn't a royal, living or dead, that hasn't had their clodhoppers cushioned by the grasses.'

Oak looked put out. 'Yes, yes. But that's enough! There will be no pleas of having royal connections. That is final.'

Thistle looked dejected. 'Yon *mannie* that protected the bonny wee flowers should be made to class *all* wild flowers the same. Either all protected, or none. It isnae fair! He singles out some plants at the expense of others. Everyone in my group has flowers, but they're no all showy. It's speciesism, just like poor Knottie said afore.'

'Well said, Thistle. The same goes for us grasses. We have flowers, though you wouldn't know it to see how we're treated.'

'There are limits,' Oak said. 'We are hardly in a position to demand that they take away the special protection of some plants. After all, we are fighting for *more* rights. Rose, Group 6, you're next.'

Thistle sat down, stuck out his spines to show his displeasure.

'I have a question first. Our wild roses in my group?'

'Certainly not! They are classed with the climbers and ramblers.'

Rose smiled, allowed her petals to shimmer. 'That's all right, then, because ... much as I wouldn't want to speak ill of anyone, I have to admit that she does have a bad reputation...'

Oak rapped the table. 'Please let's proceed. Do you have a point?'

'Well ... I ... that is... I think everything has been covered.'

'Wallflower, speak up for Group 5.'

She stood as tall as her species would allow. '*I* prefer to be known as *Cherianthus.*'

'Listen to Miss High and Mighty...'

'Grass!'

'In actual fact,' Wallflower continued, 'my full title is *Cherianthus* "Scarlet Bedder" and...'

Grass guffawed. 'Scarlet woman more like! I bet you've slept in a good few beds.'

Oak stood, banged the table. 'Grass! That's enough! This conference is about gaining respect for *every* plant. Do you have any comments, Wall ... er *Cherianthus?*'

With inflamed cheeks, she sat down, turned her face to the wall.

'Let's press on then. Chrysanthemum, Group 6, your views, please.'

'I have nothing to add, we are happy to go with majority decisions.'

'I should think you are, oh flower of the Far East.' Grass couldn't help giggling. Well, he thought, their ancestry needs bringing out.

Oak glared at the offender.

'What? I haven't said anything.'

'May I remind you,' Oak said in his sternest voice, 'that your own origins have never been proved conclusively.'

'Don't talk so daft. Everybody knows that Britain has the greenest grass, the *best* grass. So we must have started here. Stands to reason.'

Oak rustled his leaves. 'As far as I am aware, the origin of the species does *not* include the origin of grass. Therefore, you are an unknown quantity, and most probably of foreign extraction.'

Grass gave him a withering look, his blades turned red. 'You've got a nerve! Call me a foreigner! If you're going back to creation, mate, then we're all foreigners, the whole bleed'n' lot of us.' Then he remembered: *Lose your temper ... lose the argument.* That's what Elephant Grass always says ... and elephants never forget. He took a gulp of air to calm his anger. 'And you in particular, *Mr* Oak, have more recent connections abroad. Cork Oak is indigenous to Portugal and Spain. So three guesses as to whose ships your group planked during the Spanish Armada!'

Oak's bark lost its definition, lost some colour.

'Daffodil, Group 3.' His voice had taken a downward tone.

Serves him right, Grass thought. He isn't up to the job.

'Everything that concerns me has already been said.' Daffodil fluttered her petals and sat down.

And you escaped, my girl, Grass thought. If you'd started blowing your own trumpet about being Welsh, I'd have marked your card.

'Group 2, that's you, Orchid, my dear,' Oak said as he practically bowed to the South American beauty.

'I speak about bad treatment...'

Grass stood up. 'Right! I've had enough of this. She and her kind have *special* treatment...'

'No, no, Señor Grass,' Orchid said. 'You no understand. They bring us to this country. We like. Is good place, nice peoples. In my group some go Eden Project, receive very good care. Some go Kew Gardens and others specialists places...'

'So,' Grass said, 'What's your problem?' Just because she was attractive, and called him "señor" he wasn't going weak at the culms. At least not until after the meeting was over. Then ... well, who knows?

'Is problema for ... how you say? Plantas exóticas. Humans no understand our needs. They forget open window ... we suffocate and die. They give too little water, or too much ... we die. They give too much sun, or no sun ... we die.'

'Oh dear,' Oak said. 'This does seem to be a serious issue for exotic plants.'

Grass harrumphed. We all know that you fancy having her up in your branches.

'Untrained humans must not own exotic flowers.' Oak, for the first time since the start of the meeting, looked in the prime of foliage. 'I think we can take that as a definite clause. Is there anything else, my dear?'

Orchid smiled in a coy seductive way. 'No mas problemas, señor.'

Grass shuffled in his seat. He didn't like the way things were going with Orchid and Oak. The minute the meeting finished, he vowed to make his move.

'And now we come to my group,' Oak said as he rose to his feet. 'Group 1 comprises all species of trees, with the exception of fruit trees. Our problems are many and varied...'

'I thought they might be.'

Oak scowled. 'As I was saying before I was rudely interrupted ... our problems are many and varied, but basically we all have much in common. However, some of *you* can recover from ill treatment. Many trees cannot regenerate. Also there is the special problem for us ... that is the length of time we need to grow to maturity. We therefore need special consideration...'

Grass spluttered, stood up. 'Like as hell, you do. It might take longer for you to grow up, but when you get there look how long you live. Some of you have been around for hundreds of years – yes, brothers and sisters – hundreds of years, for just one plant. What about the annuals and biennials? They only get either one or two years. Think yourself lucky, mate.'

Thistle shook his head. 'Aye, its no kind of leader as puts himself first.'

Taps on the table, nods and mutterings confirmed Grass's views. As for Grass, he noticed that some of Oak's acorns were shaking themselves free. No doubt they were ashamed of their father's comments.

'Order, order.' Oak rapped on the table. 'We have completed our requests...'

'Demands,' Grass said. 'It's no use being sissified over this. They are demands.'

Without warning, Thistle stood up. 'Hang on a wee while. Oak, have ye no forgotten some of our brethren?'

Oak's branches drooped. 'No, I'm sure I have accounted for everyone.'

'Aye! What about yon fungi?'

'Fungi!' Oak frowned. 'Don't be absurd! If we included fungi then the lichens and algae would want to be included. Where would that lead? The moulds would demand entry, then...' Oak laughed. 'The bacteria would claim rights. Stuff and nonsense.'

Thistle maintained his stance. 'That's specisism! And it cannae be tolerated. You said so yourself.'

Oak regained his composure. 'You fools! Humans will never pass any Bill that protects bacteria. Bacteria attack humans, even kill them. It is apparent that you need my intelligence to carry our demands through.'

'So now ye challenge our intelligence.' Thistle bristled. 'I can tell ye, laddie, that...'

'That's enough, Thistle. As chairman of this meeting, I will have you banished if...'

'Banished, is it? And to where were ye intending to banish me?'

'So now its racism as well as ageism and speciesism,' Grass said. 'You climb up in your high branches and try to lord it over us. 'It's one law for you and another for us. Brothers and sisters ... Oak isn't fit to lead us. He isn't interested in *our* rights, only his own.'

Oak seemed to have taken a shaking, lost some of his pomposity and his leaves were beginning to discolour and curl.

Grass knew when to strike. He took to his feet. 'So, brothers and sisters, what shall we call this list of demands?'

'Ye could call it "The Act of Union".'

'We don't want unification with the humans, besides, I think it's been tried.'

Chrysanthemum raised his hand. 'What about Parity for Plants?'

'Good! But there isn't enough *oomph* to it. We need

something with *oomph*, something they won't be able to ignore.' Grass stood proud. 'We demand respect, to be treated with dignity and due consideration. In other words, brothers and sisters, we demand to be treated humanely.'

Thistle stood up, his prickles waved excitedly. 'I have it! I have it! We call yon demands: The Humane Rights Act.'

THE ROWAN TREE

If she had told the agent that Scottish country folk planted rowan trees to guard against witchcraft, he'd only have laughed. One of the old names for the tree was *witchen*. She wouldn't openly admit to being superstitious. Level headed, running her own business, she didn't brook foolishness. She shuddered. This house, it seemed, was her weak spot. Nobody deliberately invited evil spirits, she reasoned, yet with the rowan gone, she felt vulnerable to their ghostly presence.

The long fingers of dusk stalked the daylight. She peered out of the window. Birds squawked, flocked ready to roost. They seemed to stop mid-flight. She gazed in horror. They formed a ghostly image of a witch on a broomstick. In a flash they were once more climbing, whooping and swooping, creating a multitude of shapes. One bird broke free. Dived straight for the window where she was standing. She leapt sideways. The bird's beak cracked straight into the window.

Meredith remembered the roughness of the ragged tree stump, discovered when she moved in that morning. Remembered the dread curdling at the bottom of her stomach. They'd promised not to damage the tree.

'How could you?' she had screamed at the agent.

He had looked blank, uncomprehending.

That night, winds howled. They screeched round the windowless westerly side. Her house moaned, complained. It was defenceless. The small lamp she kept burning in her bedroom cast ghostly shadows on the walls. Surely the house can't be afraid, she thought.

She laughed at her own stupidity, a hollow laugh that echoed round the uncarpeted room. Stacked boxes, holding her unpacked clothes, seemed to mock her. Whistling winds shrieked down the chimney, demanded admittance. Only the Aga stove kept them at bay; there was no fireplace to encourage access. Defeated, they whipped up a fury throughout the night. She barely slept.

Next morning, she looked at the damaged window. It took little imagination to turn the short diagonal crack into a broomstick. The even smaller cross-cracks became the riding witch.

The wrong needed to be put right. She brought in men with a digger to excavate the stump. Then she ordered the largest rowan available. The nursery promised to deliver it, together with several bags of compost to give it a good start.

She had returned to her roots. Hardly able to contain her joy when she saw the property advertised for sale. Two centuries ago, her ancestors built this two-roomed croft, a *but and ben* to the locals. At her request, the builders extended it to include the steadings. The enlarged single storey stone house was beautiful, but naked without the obligatory rowan. It was September; the tree should have been alive, scarlet-berried clusters weighing down its branches.

All day, small flocks of birds congregated. Chattered on the roof. Scolded from the fences. They made diving sorties over Meredith and the workmen. She shivered and retreated inside. Reason told her it could simply be that she had deprived them of their autumn feast of berries. She couldn't listen to reason. Its cold values didn't calm her nerves.

Eventually, after severing the lower roots, the digger gouged the stump out of its resting place. While she was inside, unpacking, they had dumped the excavated soil haphazardly, top soil mixed with subsoil.

She paced nervously as she waited for her replacement tree. They'll be along "just now", the woman had said over the phone. In her naivety, she took this to mean prompt delivery: that morning, the afternoon at the latest. There was no reply to her repeated calls. The tree didn't arrive.

Meredith had closed the curtains before dusk. Left the birds to perform their aerial acrobatics unwatched. In a half-hearted attempt to shut everything out, she locked and bolted the doors.

Around six o'clock, there was a deathly stillness. The wind had abated. Probably catching its breath for renewed onslaught, she thought, as she dreaded another unprotected night. The wind crept round the western corner of the house. Then blew gustily and noisily. She heard cries from outside and flipped on the outside light. Cautiously she opened the door. A young child's voice was calling out.

'Help me,' it said, in between its sobs. 'They're coming to get me.'

'It's all right,' Meredith said, 'I won't let anyone hurt you. Where are you? Come here, to the light.'

'Help me.'

Meredith left the light on, the door open. She slipped her coat over her shoulders. Snatched up a torch. 'Where are you?'

She walked forward, flashed the light. Called to the child. As she passed the hole and the mound of earth, there was coldness in the air, as though the polar icecap had slid south. She shivered. Pulled her coat close.

There were no further cries for help. No more wailing. Puzzled, she returned to the house. She locked and barred the door, switched off the outside light.

As she prepared for bed, the wailing started again.

'We're not safe,' the child's voice said. 'The tree has gone.'

She switched on all the lights and searched every corner. Nobody else was in the house. The crying continued. She climbed into bed. Sat up, propped against the pillows. It was the safest place, she felt. With only the stone wall behind her, nothing could creep up unseen. The wind returned. It was less furious, but brought with it torrential rain. Heard above the lashing on her windowpanes, the child wailed. All night, it begged for the comfort she was unable to give.

The next morning dawned, innocent and blue. No sign of the wind and rain. The ghostly child made no sounds, yet she could still feel its presence. Still feel it following her round, as though clinging to her skirts, as it sought her protection.

She phoned the nursery about her tree and compost. They promised delivery, "sometime today".

She inspected the hole. Although the bottom was damp, the rainwater had drained away. That was strange. The ground was heavy, on the edge of the peat bogs; there should have been a miniature pond. She shrugged. Content that at least she would be able to plant the rowan as soon as it arrived. Then something caught her eye. A pale, round shape glistened in the mound of earth. She shrank back in horror. Then edged forward, to make certain she was not imagining what she had seen. There was no mistake. It was a small skull, partially uncovered by the rain. The eye sockets stared at her, almost pleaded for her help. With shaking hands, she phoned the police.

★ ★ ★

Carefully, they examined the site. The peaty soil had preserved remnants of sacking that had once held the body of a small child.

Was this the ghost-child?

The severed tree had been mature. A lump rose in Meredith's throat, her body quivered as she thought of the parents. Maybe last century, penniless, driven by superstition, they had planted a rowan to protect their child. She knew that crofters were always replanting to replace an aging rowan tree. Even when saplings sprung up where birds had excreted the seed, nobody would have dared uproot them. To uproot, or chop down, a rowan would have brought terrible punishment. She shuddered, remembered the brutish slaughter of her tree.

'*I* didn't chop it down,' she said to the evil spirits.

Then she laughed, realised she was looking at it from the wrong angle.

'You are *pleased* it's gone, aren't you? It's *because* the tree has gone that you have access to the house.'

She smelled their presence. Felt their closeness. Feared what they could do. 'I'll put things right. I'll plant the rowan and keep you out.' She wanted to free the tiny ghost-child who was terrified, unable to rest peacefully.

The police didn't seem to suspect foul play. It was a remote area. Life had been hard. The local churchyard attested to the fact that many children had died young. They strung a cordon round hole and mound.

As promised, the nursery delivered her rowan. Sadly, she left it in its tub, waiting for the police to allow her access to the hole. Each day, the birds came.

They scolded. Dived, time and again, their pointed beaks armed for attack. At night, the ghostly child walked her house, called for help. She knew the rowan must grow *in* the earth, not be balanced on the ground. Yet, she felt, it offered some small protection. No physical ill befell her, even though she shook with anxiety. At dusk, she could feel the ghosts of the witch still circling overhead, circling and watching. Whispering in the wind. Waiting.

During the night the child wailed plaintively. 'Help me. They're coming closer.'

Throughout each night, she found no peace.

Finally the police called. There had been no foul play. The child died a natural death. She wanted to attend the Christian burial arranged for that same afternoon. After all, the child could be her own kith and kin. She would plant the tree the following day.

A police representative and the clergyman were the only other people present. They carried the tiny coffin from the church towards the graveyard. A sudden gust of wind snatched at a tree. Wrenched the trunk in half. It toppled across the open grave. Blocked it completely.

Even here, at the edge of hallowed ground, she heard the evil forces laughing. She stared at the jagged trunk. There was no sign of disease in the tree, no apparent reason for its trunk to crack.

The clergyman postponed the burial.

Meredith returned home. Was there still enough daylight left, she wondered, to complete her task?

She worked hard, mixed the best of the soil from the heap with some of the compost. Part back-filled the hole. Drove in a stout stake at a forty-five degree angle. With care, she tipped the tree from its tub. Teased free the roots and planted her rowan. She added the remainder of the compost together with more soil. Trod it in. Fastened a tree-tie securely and watered in her new protector.

At dusk, she watched the birds gather. They circled above. For a moment, she saw the witch-on-broomstick formation. Then, with much squawking, the birds dispersed. Disappeared from view.

That night, hailstones bombarded the house. The wind shrieked and howled. She ignored its whispering threats. The ghost of the child was still with her but it no longer cried out. Comforted, by the ghost-child's silence, her fears began to subside.

Next morning she rushed outside, worried the sapling might not have survived the storm. She smiled. The rowan stood proud and erect, small but powerful enough to protect the house and its occupants.

That afternoon, she attended the burial of the child. Finally, it rested in peace.

VIVA ESPAÑA

Charlie spread out the brochures. He hunched forward, stared open-mouthed at the bikini-clad girls.

'We've got to go to Spain, bro. Look at these girls.'

Dave barely glanced at the girls. 'I'd rather go to Skeggy.'

'Skeggy?' Charlie sneered. 'And how many beauties are you going to see stripped off at Skegness?'

'They have them beauty competitions. Every week.'

'Suit yourself, but I'm going to Spain.' Charlie hoped the bluff would work, because he didn't fancy going alone. With the last of his mates handcuffed into marriage, there was only his younger brother left. Charlie sighed. Dave was his opposite, tall, slim, good-looking ... a bit of a babe-magnate. Trouble was he never got the hang of chatting them up. He'd given his young brother the benefit of his experience, and even more extensive knowledge of what *didn't* work, but Dave couldn't cotton on.

'I really fancied Skeggy...'

Charlie laughed. 'You're scared of flying, aren't you?'

'Course not.'

'There's nothing to it. Piece of cake.'

Dave scowled. 'You haven't been abroad. Have you?'

'Not exactly abroad ... but I've been on the Big Dippers and that stuff. How different can it be? They take off, climb up high and then land you back at the beginning. Except of course, we'd land in Spain.'

'Would we go on one of them tour things? We'd meet some girls on the plane.'

'Where's the point in that? We want Spanish girls, don't we?'

'So why have you got all them magazines about tour holidays?'

'You blind or something? To check out the talent, of course. But we're not paying their prices. I've been on the Internet. Found a good deal, and a cheap flight.'

Dave starting tapping his feet, a sure sign that his excitement was mounting. Charlie sighed in relief since he'd already bought the tickets and booked the apartment.

Then Dave's bottom jaw dropped. 'I can't go. I haven't got no passport.'

'Sure you have, bro. I got it for you. Remember last winter when we took those photos in that booth? Remember when I asked you to sign your name? With a flourish, Charlie produced their passports. 'Ta-da!'

They arrived at Málaga airport mid-morning. Stood waiting by the carousel for their luggage while the various guides herded the tour groups onto waiting buses.

'That could have been us, Charlie. We could've been on our way.'

'Well that's where we're one up on that lot of losers.'

'I don't get yer.'

Charlie puffed out his chest. 'When that lot get to their hotel, where do you think their luggage will be? I'll tell you. Right here, along with ours. They'll still be waiting when we're in our apartment, *with* our cases.'

But their suitcases didn't appear on the first slow spinning trip, or the second. Two hours later, the carousel kicked into action, yet again.

Dave leapt to his feet, danced up and down and pointed. 'There! That's mine.'

He claimed his bedraggled grey case with its distinctive twin red ropes tied where the locks should have been. When Charlie's case finally arrived, they discovered there were no buses. In the heat of the sun, the height of fiesta time, a solitary taxi sat, as though glued to the otherwise deserted tarmac. The driver was slumped in his cab, cap tilted down over his face.

Charlie rapped on the window. 'Torremolinos! And make it snappy.'

The driver woke with a start. He didn't move, but with his thumb indicated towards the rear. They loaded their own suitcases. Then Charlie gave him the slip of paper bearing their holiday address.

Their destination seemed to have been side-streeted. For them there were no whitewashed walls with shining red roofs. A greyish-green building skulked down a narrow alley. Both ground and second floor bore a rusting iron balcony that ran the full length of the building.

They lugged their baggage from the boot.

Charlie took out his wallet. 'How much?'

'You have Euros?'

Is he a nut case, Charlie thought. We've only just got off the plane, how could we have Euros? He shook his head.

The driver shrugged. 'In pounds, is more. Is hundred pounds.'

'You what! Hundred quid! I'm not *buying* your rattle-trap taxi.'

'Is hundred pounds.' The driver stared hard. Then shrugged his shoulders. 'You no pay, I radio *policía*, you have holiday in jail.'

'It's a rip-off, a bloody rip-off,' Charlie muttered as he peeled off the notes.

Dave looked round the building. 'How do we get in? There isn't no office.'

Charlie smiled. 'That's where the clever stuff comes in, see. I've got the number of our apartment. Like the info said, it will be open, waiting for us. It's trust that counts, bro. Instinct and trust.' He looked at his printed-off booking sheet. 'We're in twenty-seven.'

True to Charlie's expectations, the door to twenty-seven was unlocked. They went in. Were about to try out the beds when two lads walked in.

Charlie didn't understand a word of their gibbering.

'Twenty-seven. That's us.' He pushed the sheet in their face. 'See.'

The lads didn't seem to see the funny side. '*Estúpido.* This twenty-one.' One youth pointed to the last digit on his door. 'Twenty-one. Is one ... no seven. You go!'

So why, Charlie thought, did it have a tail on it like a seven?"

He counted the numbers up, reached twenty-seven. Then saw that the seven on their door had a line drawn horizontally across it.

Charlie walked in, flung his case on the floor.

'That's daft, if you ask me.'

Dave closed the door. 'Where's the key?'

'How the hell should I know?'

'There isn't no key.'

They searched the room. No key ... and nobody in authority to ask.

Charlie played it cool, looked disinterested. 'Makes no odds.' There was no way he was going back to enquire at number twenty-one.

Apart from that inconvenience the place wasn't bad. The main room was spacious, with two single beds and when he wandered through the archway, he discovered a kitchenette and bathroom. Then his stomach rumbled.

'We leave our gear in our cases and shove the cases under the beds. Then we pull down the covers. Easy! Come on, Bro, I'm starving.'

They stopped at the nearest café. Studied the menu.

'I just want egg and chips,' Dave said.

Charlie thought for a moment and decided it would probably be the safest thing. He looked round for inspiration. No fried eggs or chips decorated the many posters. He flapped his arms, clucked. Then, making the shape of an egg with his fore-finger and thumb, said, 'Eggs ... fried and chips.'

How the hell do I make like a chip, he thought.

The bartender shrugged. '*Patatas fritas con huevos.*' Charlie gaped. '*Patatas* with eggs, everything fried, for the English.'

'Sounds about right,' Charlie muttered to Dave. Then raised his voice. 'Two lagers.'

They wolfed down their meal, washed it down with a few lagers and were about to leave, when two girls approached them.

'You sexy English boys,' one said, 'you want much fun tonight?'

She was a knockout. Charlie couldn't believe their luck. 'Yes, darling, we want fun.'

'We come to your apartamento tonight. We come late, have much fun.'

The girl bent down, ran her finger down Charlie's thigh and kissed his cheek. '*Hasta luego.*'

Charlie was already drooling. Dave's jaw dropped, his eyes widened, pupils dilated.

'Told you, didn't I? They're just begging for it.' Charlie rubbed his hands in anticipation.

After a stroll round the town, and a few more bevvies, they returned to their apartment. Their cases were where they left them, and untouched. Charlie rifled through for his best T-shirt and jeans, slung them across his bed, the one by the outer door. They showered, shaved, slapped on aftershave ... and waited. During the day, the heat had built up and now in the thick night air, it was unbearable. Charlie drew back the curtains, opened the window.

Visitors arrived. But not the kind that they were expecting. Charlie swatted his neck and then his arm, followed by his face. 'Bloody mozzies. They're eating me down to the bone.'

'They're not bothering me,' Dave said.

Charlie jumped up, closed the window, and redrew the curtains. With all the lights on he set about swatting the mosquitoes. He was sweating and covered in swelling bites by the time he declared the place safe.

Dave's shoulders drooped. 'They're not coming, are they?'

'No, they're not. Who cares? I'm ready for a night's kip anyway.'

It was too hot for pyjamas, too hot for bed sheets. They flopped, naked, onto their respective beds and soon fell asleep.

Charlie was disturbed from a dream about sun-drenched beaches and a beautiful girl by real-life lips exploring his face. He could feel an arm round his shoulder as the lips continued their search. Now fully awake, fully alert, he put his arm round his visitor, felt her fur coat.

How the hell can she wear a fur coat in this heat, he thought. 'Take your coat off, love.'

'Ooh, ooh ooh.'

These foreign babes are something else, he thought, she must be really keen. He ran his hand upwards. His fingers found a furry head, large ears...

He yelled as if a crocodile had face-felt him. But an ear-splitting screech drowned his voice. The door swung open, let in the faint moonlight. His visitor departed swiftly, on all fours. At the door the chimp turned, it's face broadened into a grin of sorts, it gibbered some love message, and then ran off.

Dave creased up. Tears rolled down his face as he rocked with laughter. Charlie, red-faced, stood and was about to chase after whoever had played the trick when he realised that he was still starkers. He slammed the door shut. But not before a few more flying meal-seekers had entered and set about dining on various parts of his body. He leapt in bed, pulled a sheet up to his neck and turned to his brother, whose body still gave the odd convulsive giggle.

'If you breathe a word when we get back, I'll...' He couldn't think of suitable punishment. 'Just don't! Not a word! Understood!'

Dave nodded.

They woke early next morning, neither referred to the previous night's events, but Charlie was unusually quiet. 'We're getting out.'

'But we've only just got here. Our tickets say next Tuesday.'

'Not out of the country, you... Out of this apartment. I'll find us a hotel, so pack your case.'

Unbreakfasted and morose, they began to trudge the streets. Charlie spotted a hotel that displayed one of the tour company's logos.

'We should've had them cases with wheels,' Dave said as he lugged his baggage up the steps.

'No way! You want me to look a right ponce?'

Charlie sighed as he dropped his case by the reception desk. Remembering his previous efforts to portray his request, he took a different tack. 'You ... Speak ... English?'

The man nodded.

'We want one room, with two beds. One for me, one for Dave.'

'How long you stay?'

'Six days.'

'Is no possible. Stay one week, two weeks, no days.'

'But our plane leaves on Tuesday.'

The receptionist's smile, though polite was distant, uncaring. 'You go Tuesday, pay for Wednesday. Pay now.'

'Hang about! Why should we pay for an extra night?'

'I no understand. Who is this Angabout? He is with you? You want three bed in one room, or separate room?'

Charlie was losing the will to live. What is it with these foreigners, he thought, can't they speak proper English? 'One room, two beds!' He slapped the money down, held out his hand for the key. 'Can we get some breakfast?'

The receptionist nodded. 'Sí, Señor.'

Charlie turned, puffed out his chest. 'You hear that, bro. He called me senior, he knows I'm the top man.'

'Yeh! You told him.'

Charlie shoved the room key in his pocket. 'Let's fill our bellies first.'

Full of cheer and the hope of a good meal, they rushed towards the restaurant. Before opening the door, they heard the clatter of cutlery and the chatter of voices, mainly English. But what they saw as they stepped inside brought Charlie to a standstill. On almost every table there was a castle wall of cereal packets, ramparted with jars of various varieties of marmalade.

'It's like a supermarket,' Charlie said. 'Fancy having cereal and toast when there's good grub on offer.'

They soon discovered the holidaymakers' tactics. Breakfast, Spanish style, was bread rolls, an individual pot of *mermelada*, and coffee. Charlie's hopes sank. His stomach slouched in disappointment. An empty table beckoned. They put down their meagre breakfast and looked with envy at the feasting tourists.

Charlie buttered his roll, reached for the *mermelada*. Then he grinned. 'This lingo is easy.' He pointed to the jar. 'See! That's marmalade!'

'I don't think it's marmalade,' Dave said as he took his first bite. 'And it says: *m-e-r-m-e-l-a-d-a p-e-c-h-e* on the jar. What's *peche*?'

Charlie was already pulling a face. 'Who knows? It tastes like peaches! But what nut case would put peaches in marmalade? Where's the thick-cut?' Then a thought struck him. 'If they only have rolls for breakfast, I bet they have a blow-out at dinnertime.'

'But we aren't booked in for us dinners.'

'I know that! But if *these* have a good dinner, then it follows that wherever we go there will be plenty.'

With this thought in mind, they walked through the town, intending to find the beach. A bar waylaid them. They grinned at each other and marched in, ordered their lagers and took them to the outside tables. All was quiet, and content for a while, then Dave nudged his brother.

'Look! There, across the street. It's them two girls. The ones we thought we'd pulled.'

Charlie looked. Saw that the girls had company.

'Hey!' Dave was tapping his feet, setting his knees bouncing. 'It's the lads from the apartment. Look! Look at that chimp, all done up in a dress. I bet it's that...'

But Charlie had made a quick getaway, left Dave talking to himself. There was no way he wanted reminding about his hairy visitor of the previous night. Now he knew that those creeps were involved, he felt murderous. He needed revenge. Although how he could achieve that without further humiliation was beyond his imagination. Dave's arrival interrupted his thoughts.

'What you go off for?'

Charlie turned on his brother. 'I told you before. Button it! Not a word. I'm warning you!'

This holiday was not going as planned, Charlie thought with a sigh, and he realised that they had spent more than if they'd booked a package holiday. Then he spotted another bar. A bar with food piled high on the counter. He swerved off course, almost brought Dave to his knees.

The bottles of spirits caught Charlie's eye. 'That's what we need. Something to buck us up.'

He pointed to the Vodka. 'Two!'

They stared at the food on display. And then moved in, started scoffing at an alarming rate. Two more vodkas were ordered, and then two more. And so their gorging continued, the vodka keeping pace with the tapas.

'Hey, look!' Dave held up a colourful tit-bit. 'This has got them sucker things on it.'

At the very thought, Charlie's shuddered. 'It can't be! It doesn't say "octopus" anywhere up on that board.'

'Well, like I said, it's got suckers.' Dave thrust the piece in his brother's face. 'It has, hasn't it?'

Charlie had trouble holding on to the contents of his stomach. Only another vodka saved the day. 'I reckon I've had enough.'

They walked out. A mixture of unknown food swilled about in volumes of vodka. Without a word of consultation their feet led them back to the hotel and the comfort of their room. Charlie sat on the bed. Held on to his middle. 'I've got bellyache.'

'Me an all.'

They slept. Later, Charlie prised open one eye, saw it was still daylight, and with a groan, he turned on his side. By morning, he was feeling very unwell, and glared at his brother's chirpy demeanour.

'I'm ill,' he said with a groan. 'It was that octopus that did it. Foreign muck! We should have stuck to English, and had a nice big fry-up.'

'That vodka was good though,' Dave said.

'Yep! The vodka was good. I reckon that was what saved us. If we hadn't drunk so much, we'd have been at death's door by now.'

Charlie spent the remainder of the week in bed, ordered Dave about, demanded water, dry toast, or whatever took his fancy.

On the last full day, he felt sufficiently recovered to venture out.

'I've had a brilliant idea,' Charlie said. 'I know how we can get some of our money back.'

'Are we gonna sue that bar for poisoning you?'

'Nah! Though we should, it would serve them right,' Charlie said, but wondered whether or not to keep that option in reserve. 'We buy half a dozen bottles of vodka. Now I know it's so good, I think we've been missing out all these years. And here's the clever bit ... we put three in your case, three in mine. Customs will never suspect anything.'

They bought the vodka, packed it in with their dirty clothes. Once they, and their cases, were safely aboard the flight home, Charlie grabbed Dave by the arm, pulled him closer.

'I've had a brilliant idea for next time. Next time we get one of them rent-a-heap cars. We go under the tunnel, nip across that bit of France and down to the Spanish coast.'

Dave frowned. 'I don't follow. Why would we do that?'

'Well, here's the clever bit. We take our clothes in carrier bags. *Coming back,* we load the boot and the back seat with cartons of vodka, sling some clothes over the top ... and we're home and dry. *And* we'd have a car to attract the girls.'

Dave's eyes rounded. 'That's real good, that is. But why haven't them tourists done it?'

Charlie thought for a minute. 'Because they all go on package holidays, that's why.'

After landing, they collected their cases and Charlie walked through customs with an air of total innocence. Dave looked his usual self, which seemed to be sufficient for them to pass through unmolested.

Back at Charlie's, Dave unfastened the ropes on his case. Plunged in his hand. 'It's all wet.'

'You didn't wrap them up proper. A bottle's got broken.'

But when they investigated, all three bottles were smashed. Charlie unlocked his case, found an equally soggy mass, and ... three more broken bottles.

'It's them bloody men at customs. I bet they dropped our bags deliberately just to stop us having our booze.'

Dave stood, downcast, still pale-skinned and now, empty-pocketed.

Charlie glared at him. 'I told you we should have gone to Skeggy. But you wouldn't listen, would you?'

'But it was me that...'

'Next time, we do it my way.'